Dan Scannell

The Fall of a Sparrow

Black Rose Writing | Texas

I wish to express my thanks to Dr. David L.Rogers of Kingston University and Dr. Susan Fay, formerly of Marymount University, for their encouragement and guidance.

Most of all, I extend a heart felt thanks to my wife, Laura, and my daughters, Susan and Sarah, for their patience, their faith and their unstinting efforts, without which this book would never have seen the light of day.

Map of Paris, 1557: Isle de la Cité, Notre Dame

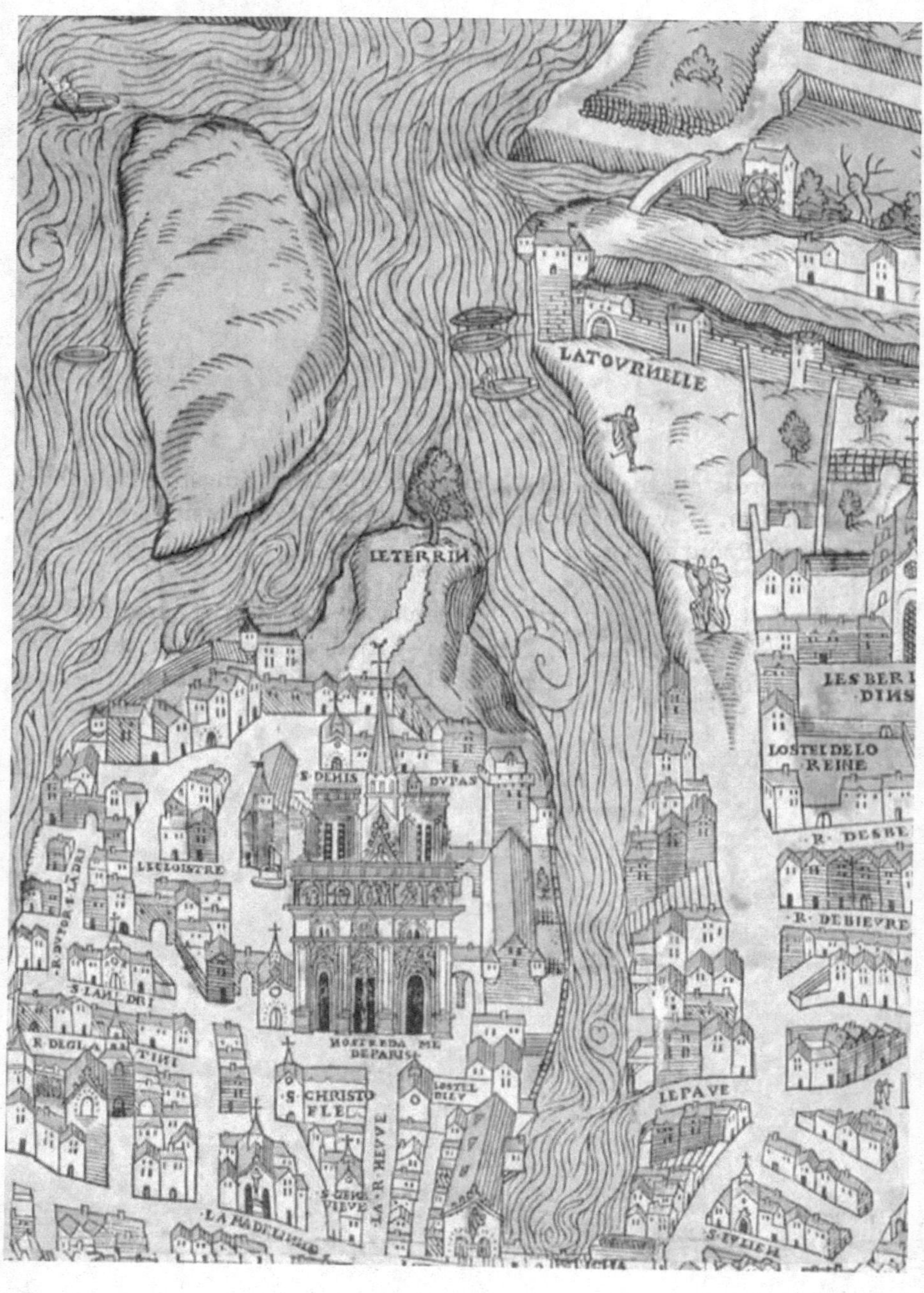

Map of Paris, 1557: Latin Quarter, showing the Collège du Cardinal Lemoine

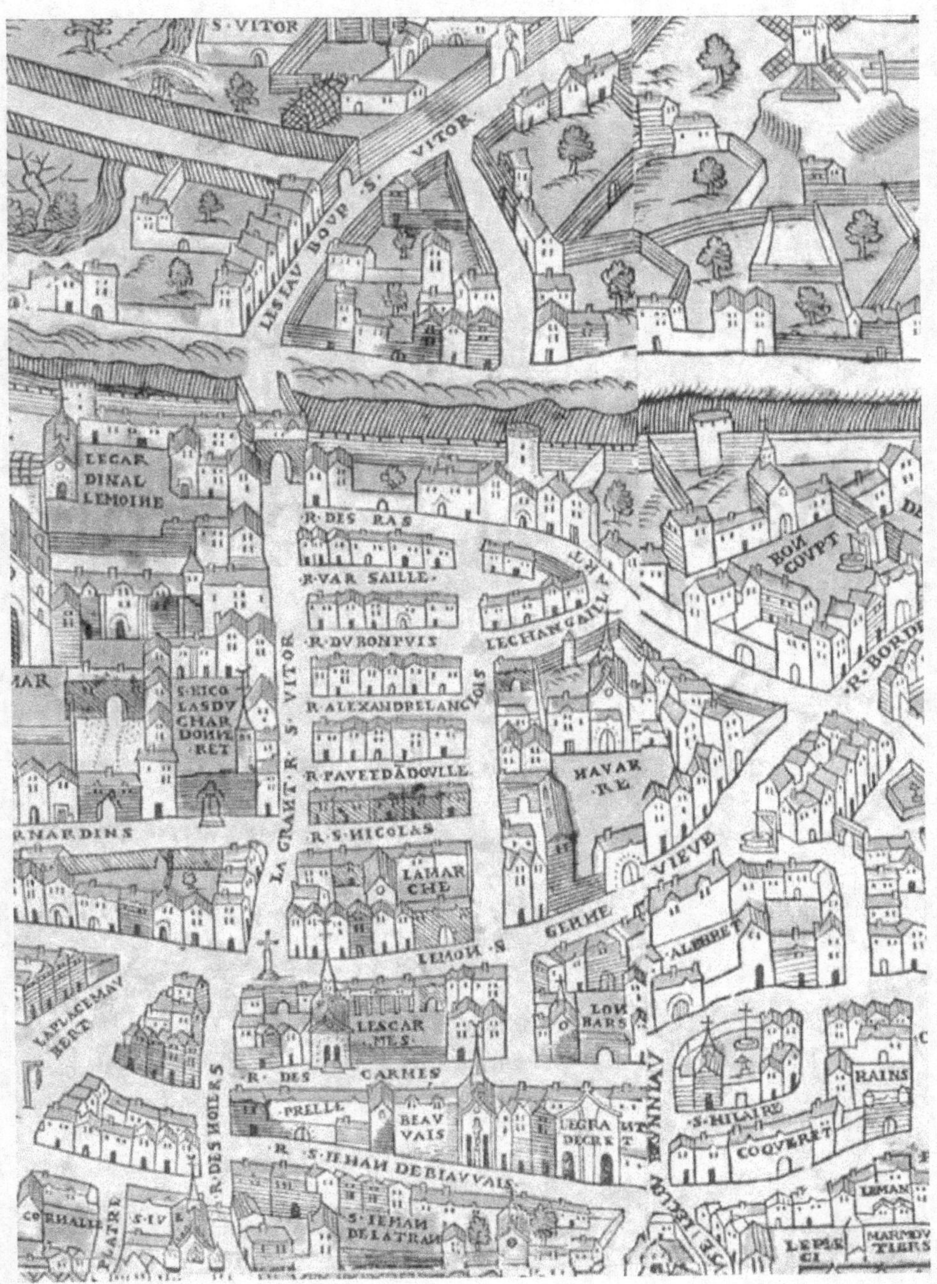

The Fall of a Sparrow

"…There's a special providence in the fall of a sparrow;"
William Shakespeare (Hamlet V, ii 220-221)

Prologue

December 12, 1546 – Reigate Castle, Surrey, England

A young boy was playing archer, guarding one of the tower's narrow windows, when he caught sight of what must have been a messenger arriving shortly after noon. The cloaked rider's grey and winded horse snorted and panted billows of smoke into the gathering chill, and the youngster could clearly hear the sound of iron shod hooves clacking on the cobble stoned path from the drawbridge. Despite the bitter weather, both rider and horse were visibly flushed and perspired, having travelled in great haste, for a considerable distance. Always observant and with a keen eye for detail, the boy concluded, from the rider's pointed shoes and tilted, flat cap, that he had ridden all the way from London.

After a sharp rap upon the door and a brief conversation with the porter, the rider, who had received strict orders to deliver his message in private only to the master, was escorted without ceremony into the presence of Henry Howard, Earl of Surrey.

Howard knew full well that his friends had scattered like grass seeds to the wind, once it became known that he had fallen from the King's grace. Although there were not many who would admit to being his friend, there were more than a few who hated Edward Seymour, the Earl of Hertford, as much as he did. One such enemy of his enemy was also his brother-in-law, John de Vere (Uncle John), the Earl of Oxford. De Vere heard from a reliable source that the Privy Council had issued warrants for both Surrey's arrest and that of his father, Thomas Howard, the Duke of Norfolk. It was said that the King had placed his seal on both warrants the previous morning and that the Duke was already in custody. At great risk to himself, de Vere had dispatched a trusted servant to Reigate to warn Surrey.

Much to the rider's astonishment, The Earl appeared more perplexed than surprised by the news. He seemed oddly relieved, perhaps even satisfied with the sudden finality of it all. Surrey grunted his gratitude and dispatched a servant to see to the messenger's mount. Remembering himself, he ordered another servant to escort his weary guest to the kitchens for a tankard of ale and a warm bowl of mutton stew.

Left alone to digest this long foreseen intelligence, Surrey withdrew to his study, in the familiar company of his books, to consider his options. He now knew how his enemies were going to move against him and how soon they would strike. The more he thought about it, the more furious he became. The charge of treason was patently absurd. As he paced the flag stones of the spare, almost Spartan room, whose only furnishings were a row of chests, labelled and filled with manuscripts, a small, table-like desk and one armless, straight backed chair, he glanced up at the formal portraits of his war-like ancestors. The Howards had served the crown with pride for over 350 years. Theirs was royal blood, after all! He observed, with a smirk of self-satisfaction, that the shield, cut into one of those ancient frescos, depicted the three golden lions of the Plantagenet dynasty.

The trial, if there was to be one, would be a sham. It would be quick and sure like the thrust of a sword. Nevertheless, all that now remained to set this ludicrous chain of events into motion was for there to be another visitor from London to serve the warrant.

Dismissing it all with a shake of the head, Surrey turned his attention to the present, calling an immediate conference with his wife, Lady Frances, their 11 year old son, Thomas, and his chief steward, Will Townsend. No, he would not flee to Scotland or to France. There clearly wasn't time, and besides, Howards do not run in the face of danger. He wanted to inform the younger children that he might be going away for a while, but Lady Frances insisted that they be kept out of it.

"You'll frighten them to death for no good reason. This will all pass; you'll see. The King's been furious with your father many times, but they've always reconciled. He will repent his fit of anger and recall the warrants. Everyone will be preparing for Christmas and the whole thing will be totally forgotten by the New Year, if we can only just stay out of sight for a while."

Surrey waived the idea away with an outstretched hand. "This time is different. The dogs have scented blood, and they will only be satisfied with the kill."

What Lady Frances didn't realise was that one of the younger children, her seven year old son, Henry, the one who had been playing sentry when the messenger arrived, had been with his brother when the latter received his summons to meet with their father. Young Henry had followed at a distance and was listening outside the door. He didn't fully understand what a warrant was or where his father might be going, but he could tell that it was not good news. The adults were always whispering in secrecy. He hated their secrets! He had to find out what they didn't want to tell him.

A cold rain began to fall at around three o'clock that afternoon, soaking the ground and permeating the dank air. Darkness descended rapidly over England, as the decaying year plodded inexorably toward its end. Even the dwindling daylight hours were dim and colourless. A bitter, northerly wind screeched and howled like a widow at the gallows, driving leaves and drizzle in sweeping circles against the narrow windows of the castle.

Normally, despite the weather, there would still be the buzz of excitement in the air, well into the darkening hours. The Earl and Lady Frances always insisted on having an early family holiday feast with the children before going off to Whitehall for Christmas with the King. Their servants would ordinarily be busy late into the evening with cleaning and decorating for the event. This year, however, there was only the cold stillness of waiting, interminable waiting for the sound of approaching horses and a percussive knock at the door.

They took their supper as a family, as was their custom, but the table was uncharacteristically muted. Earl Henry tried to put on a cheerful face, but Lady Frances was clearly troubled and distracted. The meal concluded almost without conversation, and then there was more whispering and murmuring in the parlour before Lady Frances called the nanny to put the children to bed. The young boy, Henry, walked slowly and lingered in the hallway long enough to overhear his mother say: "If only we can remain undisturbed tonight, we just might make it." In that instant, the child was seized by a violent chill, goose bumps on his arms and the back of his neck. He was certain (he didn't know how) that his father would not get that peaceful night. Reluctantly, he went to bed, but not to sleep.

The boy tossed and turned until the bed clothes came completely undone and were all twisted in ribbons and tossed in a heap on the stone floor. Unable to pretend to sleep any longer, he arose as noiselessly as he could and took hold of a pewter candle stick that was on his night table. Just outside the door of the room he shared with his older brother, who clearly had no trouble sleeping through all of this, he stretched on his toes to light the candle from a wall sconce. Pressing himself as close as possible against the wall, he made his way downstairs, concealing himself behind the large pillars that supported the roof and separated the rooms. As the hushed voices in front of him came closer and closer, he paused, blew out the candle and then held his breath for a minute or so, until he was sure that he was undetected. Looking around, he found concealment behind the curtain that separated his father's study from the hallway leading to the room where his parents received guests in times past. His father was speaking rapidly to Townsend.

"Here is a list of the deeds for all of the tenants. This mark (You see, here?) next to a name indicates whether or not each has paid his rent for the year."

"Yes, milord."

"Lady Frances is to have absolute authority to deal with the tenants, as well as with all of my debtors and creditors. You will take orders only from her."

"Yes, milord."

"Dear Frances, you will take the children and go to some place safe. Don't come anywhere near London or try to visit me in the Tower. They will be quick. They have to be. The King, they say, is seriously ill. He uses a stamp because his right side is immobile and he cannot even write his name."

"No! I won't let them have you! Command the sentries to raise the drawbridge. We can hold out for days...weeks with the provisions already secured for Christmas."

"No. I will not impede the officers of the King. There is to be no resistance. I'm responsible for everyone who lives and works here. We will give them no pretext for slaughter."

"...but what's to become of us?"

"They wouldn't dare to harm you; they have no cause. Above all, you must keep the children safe. Our sons carry the Howard name..."

Surrey was interrupted in mid-sentence by a commotion of voices and the thunder of hooves over the drawbridge. Townsend peered out of the window slit to the outside and spotted seven men on horseback, three carrying spears and two holding up torches. One led a saddled horse without a rider. Their leader, his jewelled sword clanking at his side, rode in front, on a white war horse richly decked out with a silver bridle and a tasselled silk cover on his saddle. The man himself was wrapped in furs, against the cold, over which he sported a stylish flat cap of red silk embroidered with a spray of fine jewels that sparkled like a fresh snowfall. In fact, the rain was just then turning into snow, and when the leader and two lancers dismounted, the ground upon which they lighted sprayed up slushy solids over their boots and hose. Townsend grinned darkly, when he saw them slide about for a moment before regaining their footing. The leader stepped forward with great authority and ceremony, and began to hammer at the thick oaken door using the blunt end of one of the pikes, which he grasped in his gloved fists.

Once, twice, three times, the night stillness was shattered by the horrible, cracking sound of wood against wood. The heavy door vibrated like a tuning fork and set off a sympathetic, rhythmic shuttering in the walls and floor boards throughout the keep. The tremor continued even after the pounding had stopped.

There followed another wave of repeated, resonant pounding. With each ear splitting contact, the door began to vibrate anew, and the whole anteroom of the castle became an echo chamber, augmenting the low vibrating sound like a giant drum.

The earthquake-like tremor struck again with an even stronger shock, but the Earl returned to his desk and gave the intruders no notice. A silence fell, broken again by the same insistent pounding. Townsend looked anxiously at his master to secure permission to respond to it and make it stop.

Once again, the intruder's pike struck with a vengeance. The whole house was rattled and tumbled awake. The sound was everywhere, but the shaking of that which should have been solid and unyielding was even more terrifying. Lady Frances dispatched a servant to tell the younger children to stay in their rooms.

Each period of deafening stillness was punctuated by the resumption of even more insistent pounding. This time, the hammering was followed by a hoarse and impatient voice bellowing: "Open, in the name of the KING!"

The pounding resumed with a vengeance. The mounting noise was like the sharp report of cannon. The rooms of the keep and their contents shook again in morbid sympathy with the pulsating boom.

From the stairwell emerged Surrey's elder son and heir, Thomas, holding a sword that was much too big and heavy for him to wield. He was intercepted by Lady Frances who took the sword out of his hand and placed it on the table next to the Earl. Lady Frances pulled the boy into position with her, behind his seated father.

"OPEN, I command you, in the King's name!"

Surrey dipped his quill and continued to write in an unhurried and disinterested manner. Still the pounding continued. The seismic movements of the floor and walls were even more sickening than the horribly amplified noise.

Townsend could finally take no more. "For God's sake, you'll wake the dead with your knocking!" Still, the rhythmic bursts of sound and motion continued.

With each knock, the seven year old boy shook from behind the curtain, as if his bones would shuffle off the muscle, flesh and skin that covered them. He squeezed his eyes shut and clenched the candle stick in his hand as if it held him up and kept him from crying out. He felt the warmth of his own urine, as it streamed down his leg to the floor at his feet.

Finally, Surrey looked up, and with the slightest nod of his head, gave permission for Townsend to unbolt the door.

In stalked two lancers and the leader of the intruders, a tall, broad shouldered man impeccably dressed for one who had just ridden hard for a long distance. His clothes betokened his rank, for both Surrey and Lady Frances recognised their chief nemesis, Edward Seymour, the Earl of Hertford. The latter was brandishing a scroll from which hung an elaborately decorated seal, bearing the insignia of King Henry VIII.

Without even bothering to break the seal, inasmuch as he was unable to read the Latin anyway, Hertford addressed the still seated Earl of Surrey with undisguised contempt and complete disregard for the latter's rank, station and ancient family lineage. "Henry Howard, Earl of Surrey, I arrest you in the name of the King on a charge of high treason."

Surrey still did not stand, nor did he express the slightest regard for the nature of the charge. He looked at Hertford with a dismissive smirk and calmly addressed him, as insultingly as he could imagine, by his Christian name, rather than his title. "Why Edward, is this what brings you to my home at this ungodly hour of the night? Spare me your rhetoric and let's get on with it, then, shall we?"

Had Surrey been standing, Hertford might have slugged him with his clenched fist, but he retained his composure and official demeanour. "Please rise. You are to accompany me this very evening, after which you will be turned over to the custody of the Warden of the Tower, in whose keeping you will be subject to the King's swift justice."

Surrey rose slowly to his feet, his voice calm and controlled. "I trust myself to his Majesty's judgement and to his tender mercies, in which I confess that I have greater confidence than I place in your Lordship's custody. May I first take my leave of my family?"

"Say your 'goodbyes' quickly, for I mean us to be back in London by tomorrow morning."

Hertford wore a bored expression as Surrey and his wife moved toward each other to share a parting embrace. Suddenly, everyone turned to the sound of something metallic striking the stone floor from behind the nearby curtain. Hertford reached the curtain in one stride and pulled back the cloth barrier with his left hand, his right covering the hilt of his sword. The two lancers immediately pointed their weapons at the curtain and stopped when they saw the figure of a boy, near to tears having so given his position away. On the floor next to him rested the pewter candle stick he had carried from his bedroom.

Hertford looked amused, when he realised he was not being ambushed. "What's your name, boy," he breathed into the child's face, deliberately speaking in a loud voice to frighten him even further.

"Henry, sir, Henry Howard."

"That will be 'my Lord' to you." Hertford seemed to be relishing the chance to bully the boy. "Well then, Henry Howard. Take a good look around you; you'll never call this place 'home' again. "

Satisfied with having frightened the boy, Hertford shifted his attention to the tenderly embracing couple, as if to pass final sentence on both. "His Majesty decrees that all of your prior titles, lands and possessions are hereby forfeited to the crown, from whose bounty they originated." Both boys were looking for a cue from their father to know what they should do next. Surrey raised a finger to his mouth and silently bade them say nothing.

Since there would be no further provocation or reprisals this night, Hertford turned and bade the lancers accompany Surrey out of doors.

Surrey looked at one of the lancers. "May I take a coat against the cold?"

"You'd better," interspersed Hertford himself. "You'll need it to stay warm in the Tower. I hear it's a damp and chilly place." An ugly sneer spread across his face, and he added: "Make it quick."

Townsend produced a fur lined cloak for his master. Hastily heaving the cloak over his shoulders, Surrey followed the intruders into the blackened courtyard, soon to be swallowed by the swirling snow, the howling wind and the darkness. The younger Henry Howard stood staring at the door, too frightened and grief stricken to cry.

Chapter 1

Paris, the present day

Then it dawned on me, like a missing six letter word in a crossword puzzle. I had been staring at family pedigrees for weeks now, without taking particular note of a curious juncture of two genealogical trees that had been right there in front of my face. How could I have failed to see it until now?

My mind was on overdrive, and I must have been talking so fast that I wasn't even allowing myself enough time to take a breath, let alone pausing long enough for Hank to get a word in edgewise. We were seated at a small table in the back of an Irish pub – of all places – on the *rue des Ecoles*, a couple of long blocks down from the Sorbonne and two short blocks up from the Seine, on the left bank, across from Notre Dame. I needed to get it all out - everything that had been swimming around in my head for the last two days and nights, but Hank just sat there smiling, the slight lines around her puffed lips emphasising the ease and comfort with which she always smiled.

"Hank" is short for "Henrietta", Henrietta Claudia Wells, an old friend from graduate school, who had never forgiven her parents for giving her two such names to carry like burdens through school. Whether to escape the moniker or to pursue her destiny, she gave up a promising academic career to open up a second hand book store, just down the street from where we had agreed to meet for a couple of beers. We hadn't seen each other for ten years, since she had left for what was supposed to have been a three week European vacation, and I wasn't sure if she would be willing to put up with the old Michael Devon she had left behind.

We'd kept in touch over the years, by telephone and e-mail. I was always promising myself to take a break from teaching and writing and go to see her, but I never managed to pull myself away from my work. I'm not sure if it was my passion for literature or just a convenient excuse, but I'd always managed to be too busy for an extended vacation.

So what had she been doing while we were, so to speak, just out of reach all those years? Interspersed with her accounts of her impassioned, I would say, obsessive search for the illusive rare and neglected second hand book, she also confided in me about a couple of brief affairs, most recently with a constable at the local Prefecture of Police, whom she had met in the course of an inspection, with regard to the security apparatus protecting her shop.

"That's been over a long time," she was telling me, although she insisted on pointing out that this guy apparently had a forensic specialist's love for the kind of information you could find out about people from the books they read and handled.

I didn't want to talk about him or how he analysed documents using infrared spectroscopy. I had come here for a specific purpose, but I didn't know where to begin. For some reason, I found that the prospect of gaining Hank's approval was important to me.

"It all started innocently enough. I told you about the book I'm writing, something different from the flood of speculative drivel that's been coming out about the Earl of Oxford to mark the 400th anniversary of the death of Shakespeare. You see, while most of us hold that the actor, William Shakespeare of Stratford-Upon-Avon and the poet, William Shakespeare are one and the same person, the "Oxford" school maintains that a large body of evidence points to Edward de Vere, the 17th Earl of Oxford, as the author of the plays and poems of Shakespeare. Personally, I thought it was all just a load of elitist crap. Just the idea that the capacity for greatness comes from breeding, exclusive education and the like, is an idea I found, well, offensive. That was my opinion, anyway, but I had to take the time to study the 'Oxfordian' arguments and examine their evidence with as open a mind as I could muster."

"Do you still feel that way?" Hank's head tilting to one side, allowing her still shoulder length red hair to cascade softly over half of her face, in a way that I had always found extremely distracting.

"That they are elitists, certainly, but that there might very well have been another voice, speaking through Shakespeare's lines, I really can't say."

I shook my head as if to dismiss some arguments that were still playing out in my mind. "I had spent the better part of two months in England, much of it with faculty members at Brunel University in West London, where they offer a Masters specialisation in the Shakespeare authorship question. I made the acquaintance of Doctor James Bennet. By day, he's a famous author and lecturer in Elizabethan and Jacobean drama, but he also belongs to a group of scholars, actors and such who called themselves, 'The De Vere Society.'"

Hank's response was a derisive grunt and another swing of her copper-red hair to emphasis the point. "You mean an 'old boys' club, an excuse for stuffy old prigs to sit around drinking gin and weaving conspiracy theories!"

"Actually, Doctor Bennet turned out to be a delightful, down-to-earth sort of guy, and thoroughly knowledgeable in his field. Much to my surprise, I found the other society members, with whom I consulted on some small points, all very serious and completely respectable scholars. Still, after looking through underlined bibles and examining family trees until the lines seemed to blur before me, I found the case, while compelling, to be circumstantial and painfully inconclusive."

"You sound almost disappointed that they were not able to convince you," observed Hank, with another playful smile forming around her mouth and eyes.

"Well, I couldn't get over how much the oldest and most influential families had intermarried over the years. Of course, they were using these alliances to accumulate wealth, property and titles, always a string of titles. It was all a big power game. Blood lines and political positioning were all-important, and loyalties were sealed and assured at the matrimonial altar. Many controversial figures got away with questionable behavior and opinions because they were connected to this or that person by marriage...That's when you contacted me, to entice me down here with your little piece of news.

Hank flashed one of her self-satisfied grins. "I'm happy to be of service!"

"No, I mean it. Thank God you called! I was completely bored out of my mind, actually nodding off to sleep at the desk in my hotel room, rummaging through my notes on which families were on the rise or falling out of favour for various and sundry reasons. I was getting ready to call it quits for the day, when the phone jolted me back to the real world. The next thing I heard was the welcome sound of your voice."

"You didn't sound particularly happy to be interrupted." Hank was using that gentle, scolding tone that I suppose I never really minded so much.

"All right, I was a little grumpy and stir crazy, but hearing your voice was exactly what I needed to pull me out of my mood. You always sound the same, somewhere between empathy and mockery. You teased me about not coming to see you and your precious books, and then you made some kind of crack about how I spend all my time 'researching those dull Elizabethan sonneteers'. It was only then you told me about the book you found."

Hank straightened in her chair. She knew that the small talk was over. Her playful looks were gone, now. "Well," she began, launching her own rapid narrative, eyes wide with the remembered excitement of it. "I knew as soon as I opened it that I had happened upon something that might make it worth your while to visit me. The little thing was in a carton of books that had evidently been dumped in the attic of the parish house of *Saint Germain*. It claims to be the diary of one Henry Howard of Reigate Manor in Surrey. I made out the date on the title page to be the year 1557."

"And that was it," I burst in, no longer able to keep down my excitement. "You had stumbled on the link, the missing word without which the puzzle remains...incomplete. One of the most prominent early Tudor poets, Henry Howard, Earl of Surrey, was married to Lady Frances de Vere. The Earl of Surrey and Frances de Vere had two sons, the younger one named 'Henry', like his father."

"At least they didn't name one of their daughters, 'Henrietta.'" Hank's lips were pursed, but the smile lines around her eyes betrayed her amusement.

"The Howard children were first cousins of Edward de Vere, the object of so much scrutiny by Doctor Bennet and his associates."

"You have been looking at too many family trees." Hank tried to look severe, but I could detect the old playfulness returning to her child-like blue eyes.

"Don't you see?" I couldn't help myself, even though I could see that I was amusing Hank the more I got carried away in my earnestness. "A plausible literary connection in the de Vere heritage comes from the Howard side, a poet among a family of statesmen and soldiers."

"Where are you headed with all of this?" Hank asked, her academic scepticism coming out to counterbalance my enthusiasm.

"Maybe, just maybe, Edward de Vere DID introduce the world to what we call the works of Shakespeare, but what if the plays and poems were actually written by someone else, someone Edward de Vere knew personally and who was somehow indebted to him ?"

"That's quite a leap, even for you," cautioned Hank.

"What about the Howards?" I was now arguing my case as if my failure to convince Hank would have stopped me from pursuing my idea. "Has anybody looked at the connection with the Earl of Surrey's descendants? The Howards were arguably the most prominent family in England at the time, claiming royal ancestry, back to the 13th century. They certainly had the education and the court position that the 'Oxford school' thought so pivotal to their man's candidacy."

"I still entertained the idea that you wanted to see me and not just your Henry Howard journal," protested Hank, puffing her lips in an endearing little pout.

"Yes, yes , of COURSE I did," I added, knowing that she could see in my eyes how much I wanted to get my hands on the book, while she continued to play with me.

"I'm surprised you didn't take the next plane out." She was trying desperately to look cross with me.

"There were a couple of things I had to do first," I said, ignoring her pretended jealousy. "I hung up the phone and headed for the Tube to the British Library, where I was able to find a manuscript, dated 1583, part of a recently acquired private collection. It's a tract, entitled, '*Preservative against the Poison of supposed Prophesies*', written by this younger Henry Howard. After I dropped a few well-chosen names, I was even permitted to photocopy several pages for myself. I found more material on the Howards and how they continued to contribute heroes and the occasional traitor to their country's history. (Did you know that the commander of Elizabeth's fleet that defeated the Spanish Armada was a Howard?) Then I was ready for my next call. I set out for Brunel to meet with my new friend from the De Vere Society."

"Oh yes, the famous Doctor Bennet," joined in Hank, still pretending to be resentful of my new obsession. "Where else would you go to trot out your latest theory?"

"You were the one who had just finished telling me about a potential primary source," I protested, too involved in my story to remember she was playing with me.

"Anyway, I found Doctor Bennet in his office, behind teetering stacks of papers. I spotted his shiny bald head in the reflection given off by the spot light, which was angled toward his desk like a halo."

"'So, Michael, what have you found that is so earth shattering?' He looked amused at my having rushed in all huffing and puffing.

"'Have you considered the Howards, I mean the Earl of Surrey, who married Lady Frances de Vere?' I didn't bother to sit down in the chair opposite him, to which he pointed.

"'Surrey's not a candidate. He was beheaded by Henry VIII in 1547, three years before Edward de Vere was born. There's no connection there, and Surrey died too early to have possibly been Shakespeare. The poor bastard was only thirty years old when they executed him on Tower Green...trumped up charges, as I understand.'

"'What about Surrey's sons?' I countered, not to be so easily discouraged.

"'You mean Thomas Howard, who became Duke of Norfolk, when his grandfather died, only to get himself beheaded by Elizabeth, in 1572 for trying to marry the Queen of Scots? No, no,' he continued making a dismissive 'chirping' sound with his tongue and teeth. 'They were a great family who lost everything in three generations, because they ended up on the wrong side of the religious question.'

"'But what about the second son, Henry?' I had hit my stride and was getting to the very core of my theory. 'He survived and prospered under James I. De Vere and he were first cousins, so it's fair to assume they had contact.'

"Doctor Bennett knitted his eyebrows while searching his memory. 'They had a falling out, in 1582, over religion and politics, I think. They didn't have anything to do with each other during the two and a half decades when Shakespeare's plays first appeared.'

"I settled myself in the seat opposite Doctor Bennet's desk, and continued talking, mostly to myself. 'I was reading about that incident this afternoon at the library. It seems that de Vere denounced his cousin, reviving some old charges about his being a papist and a traitor. It threatened to embroil Howard in quite a bit of trouble, but Howard made an impassioned written appeal to the Queen herself, and the charges were, just, dropped. Why do you suppose that de Vere wanted him out of the way, at that particular time, and why did the Queen intervene in Howard's favour, especially with the history that the Howards had with the Tudors?'

"'I don't know,' answered Doctor Bennet, who had, himself, written extensively on the religious divisions that had helped bring down the Howards. 'Elizabeth had every reason to be ambivalent on the subject. Her mother, the Boleyn woman, after all, was a Howard on her mother's side, but what has any of this to do with the Shakespeare authorship controversy?'

"'Perhaps nothing,' I admitted, 'but it bears looking into.'"

"It was clear that Bennet was not about to endorse or lend credence to my Howard theory. We agreed to keep in touch, and I got out of there. I immediately made arrangement for a Friday evening departure across the Channel."

Hank flashed her eyes at the waiter and paid for our beers, while I was still spewing out my story. "I think we should get going." When she pushed her chair back from the little square table and raised herself to her full height, I noticed that the flowers running down the long, slender lines of her jeans matched the bright floral pattern of her Mexican peasant styled blouse. "The book is in my shop, just down the street."

Chapter 2
A Treasure Discovered

N ow, Hank knew as much as I did about why I simply had to see her little book, and despite her attempts at looking angry, her eyes betrayed a growing excitement at the prospects it might open.

We walked the short distance from the pub, on the *rue des Ecoles*, to Hank's book store, whose sign, in ornate script, proclaimed this to be the home of "*Livres Oubliés*" (Forgotten Books). At the door, Hank turned, her wide, blue eyes playing mischievously, as she rattled the key. "Your treasure lies within," she said with a wink.

She gave a little nudge with her shoulder, and I heard the tinkling sound of the small suspended bell, tripped by the opening of the door. We went up to the counter, and Hank began rummaging melodramatically on a low shelf, beneath the portion of counter that supported the cash register. "I have always had a secret fantasy," (she rambled on to fill the silence during her search) "about finding, in someone's old attic, some misplaced treasure - such as a first edition of John Donne's poetry or a rare manuscript of Victor Hugo or somebody - hidden among the mountains of re-cycled reading, its value unknown or unnoticed for many generations. After all, aren't many of these old attics like tiny literary grave yards, the final resting place of students' used text books and old ladies' carefully preserved prayer books and missals? Somewhere, in all that reading material, there lurks an almost silenced voice, a piece of work that wishes to be discovered and saved from oblivion. I know it's there, if I could only pick it out from among the piles of paper I'm always digging through." Then she stopped abruptly and turned to me, almost apologetically. "Look at me, going on like this, instead of producing the little treasure you came here to see." At that, she reached under the dusty counter, and pulled it out.

It was old, very old, its pages yellowed and moulded into strange shapes by the crumbling of their brown edges. The plain binding, with no embossing or even fragments of lettering, was leather, peeling and discoloured but not too brittle to be handled. "It was one of several volumes in similarly poor condition," Hank said. "They were just tossed aside in no particular order." She held it out to me, and I felt a twinge of excitement as I reached for it.

My fingers gently wrapped around it, and I very carefully cracked open the cover. The fragile binding instantly separated from the stitching. as if it were made from a spider's web, and I was careful to hold it as if it were still attached, hoping that the book would simply remember how to stay intact. I was afraid the pages would dissolve into dust in my very hands, if not from my touch then from the sudden exposure to the air. I made sure that I kept it out of direct sunlight and put as little pressure as possible on the brownish sheets.

I turned to what looked like a title page. It was not printed from type face or by any other method that I could identify. Rather, it was written with what can only be described as a calligraphic hand, using an instrument capable of making both broad and thin linear strokes and loops. The original tincture of the ink had long since faded, leaving indelible marks in a rust and dirt colour that were, in some places distinct and in others were in the process of blending with the brownish hue of the page itself. I had the impression that the ageing paper, thin to the point of transparency, like the skin of a wizened old man, was trying to absorb the pen strokes into the depths of the layers of pages as a sponge absorbs spills, eventually swallowing the words themselves into the texture and contours of the ancient book.

The words that I could still make out were in Latin, announcing "*Incipit Historia Vitae Meae in Lutetia*" ("The Beginning of the Story of My Life in Paris"), by a certain Henry Howard, of Reigate Manor, Surrey. This was the same Henry Howard I had been reading about, the son of Lady Frances de Vere and the Earl of Surrey, the poet, who had been responsible for introducing the sonnet to the English language, the same Henry Howard who had quarrelled, in 1582, with Edward de Vere, the Earl of Oxford. Then, Henry Howard must have been living in Paris in…yes, Hank had been right about the date: "MDLVII", the year 1557. Let's see, born in 1540: that would make him 17 years old at the time.

As gently as if I had been lifting a thin shelled quail's egg, I turned the page to a dated and much less elaborately penned entry. These hand written words were in a kind of English which, even without the handicap of faded ink, I understood, at first, only about as well as I had grasped the thread of the Latin text on the title page. This Henry Howard's orthography was imaginative, to say the least, but most of the words, once I had mouthed my way through the phonetic spelling, were recognisable by sound, if not by sight.

I began making a mental catalogue of certain words and what I extrapolated were their equivalents in modern English -words such as:

Yf = if
Euer = ever
Mynde = mind
Deuill = devil.

I became so engrossed in this process that I was totally unaware that Hank was staring fixedly at the book she had surrendered into my hand, like a parent at once proud and anxious as she watched her child preparing to leave home forever, in pursuit of God knows what greater destiny. I felt suddenly embarrassed. as if I were holding the hand of her only daughter and leaving for some motel where I intended to take her virginity that very night. It must have shown on my face, for Hank just smiled knowingly and raised her hand in a gesture of sad magnanimity. I could take her and do with her as I pleased, because, my need to have her was greater than Hank's need to withhold her yet a little longer. Then I was aware of how inexplicably happy Hank was for me. She glanced at the book, as if to convey to it some parting words. "Be good to him," her eyes said to it, "for when he leaves me, he takes you with him." I reached out and cupped her still child-like face under her raised chin, holding her effortless smile, as it were, in my hand. We leaned into each other, and I felt her lips brush mine, for a breathless instant. I choked back what must have looked like a nearly tearful "Thank you," and, holding the journal, like a copy of the Sacred Scriptures, in both my hands, I strode to the sidewalk, as another patron held the door for me, after opening to the tinkle of the doorbell.

I looked for the nearest side walk café and found a side table away from the street but with enough indirect light to help me make out what was readable on the fragile pages of my 450 year old diary. I wanted to know more about this Henry Howard, and his do-it-yourself spelling. With only my voyeuristic curiosity to urge me on, I started analysing variously dated entries in no particular order, trying to understand as much of his vocabulary and convoluted sentence structure as I could. I was also searching for – and not finding – a thread, a story line from what were evidently random reflections, reminiscences and brief episodes about what happened to this or that person on a particular day. I knew that this would not be easy reading, and I wasn't at all sure whether Howard had finished the account of his stay in Paris or if there remained enough readable text in this journal to allow me to divine what he had finished. I felt compelled, nevertheless, to mine the book for everything that I could get from it, and to try to fill in just enough of the gaps to be able to discover and understand what Henry Howard considered important enough to record in his journal.

Before my eyes had become too itchy and sore with straining through the faded entries, I found one passage that particularly sparked my attention. I render it now exactly as I found it, with just enough added punctuation and standardisation of the spelling to make it readily readable:

"Long and tedious were the days of June, with plenteous sun and scant hours of darkness, passed here in the quarter of students and robbed scholars, with their scrolls and tablets and throats endlessly clearing themselves of fowl fluids. On such a day did I tarry with my fine fellows, Gaudin and the dower faced Dormoy in the Cutters Tavern on *Rue Traversiere*, a stone's throw from the *St Séverin*, to settle our parched throats with a draught of the local mead.

"We spoke of our homes and the secret places where summer days pass in peace and solace, when suddenly, we saw the figure of a man in the dress of a threadbare scholar, with a pointed, red beard, edged and lined in white.

Fall of a Sparrow

He was stooped over a wooden mug, eyes half closed and lips moving, addressing words to no one, in particular, that we could see.

"'Hast thou seen, in Cutters, such a figure before?' I asked Gaudin, whilst turning my head so as to silently laugh, unseen.

"'Nay, never,' said he, making no effort to hide his own bemusement.

"'Nor I,' added Dormoy, looking more curious than entertained.

"Still kept he talking, this mysterious stranger, in a tongue neither Latin nor French, occasionally punctuating a point with a wave of the arm or a point of a finger. We tried to continue our discourse, but we could not keep from gaping at his strange demeanour and continuous muttering. Strange, in truth, he was, yet also steeped in dignity and fiery fervour. We moved ever closer, until he looked up, leaned forward and pushed three stools in our direction, drawing us into the circle of his strangeness.

"'*Je suis le Docteur Michel*,' said he. '*Mangez vous ce soir*?'

"We knew not what to say nor where to go; he fixed us so with dark eyes deep and black. I caught a glimpse of Gaudin's face which bespoke of the same amusement he might derive from a juggler at a country fair, whilst Dormoy fixed his gaze upon him with a kind of morbid curiosity. What I saw, in those black eyes, fierce and intent, was the face of one who would be our father."

***

I had no idea who these people were. (What were their names - Gaudin, Dormoy?) Nevertheless, I was fascinated by this strange Doctor Michel, and I knew I wanted to learn more about him from these tattered pages. I began to form a plan. I decided to assign myself the project of transcribing everything that I could make out from Henry Howard's 450 year old journal and defining (imposing?) some kind of order with respect to these bits of description and / or narrative, to try to string them together based on what?...chronology, themes, persons, events? I didn't know how to structure these entries, but I was determined to find a way to do it – a way that was consistent with what the young author wanted to say, in these crumbling pages.

Chapter 3
A quest, driven by curiosity

I was spending more and more time in my hotel room on the rue de la Comet or sitting at a table in the central court yard of the place. There, I was transcribing what I could decipher from Henry Howard's journal, and I was starting to piece together some early accounts of a rough channel passage from Dover to Calais and an equally uncomfortable coach ride through Amiens and Beauvais to Paris. I had to remind myself how tedious and, sometimes, dangerous this journey must have been in the mid-sixteenth century. Howard must have had an enormous amount of time on his hands to think about everything that had brought him to this moment and everything that he must have expected to encounter in Paris. His thoughts went randomly from one subject to another, as I turned the pages. This is, after all, a diary, and Howard never intended it to be published or read as a book.

Still, I had the feeling that he was skirting certain subjects that he preferred not to think about, or if he couldn't avoid thinking about them, he was endeavouring not to relive them through these pages. While Howard knew what had happened before, events that were colouring what he saw and recorded on these pages, I, the reader, didn't have a clue. I was certain that what had happened before the coach ride and before the sea journey must have contributed more to his sense of turbulence, discomfort and, perhaps, danger, than the storms crossing the Channel and the highway robbers on the road to Amiens. It wasn't until I had gotten further into the journal, to the accounts of his later conversations with his circle of friends, that I found references to events that he was finally able to confide to, of all people, this very same Dr. Michel whose name I had encountered in my first random perusal of the pages. Here is one such passage, occurring, as many of them did, in the public room of a tavern:

"'The aspect thou wearest is distracted and distant this evening, young Howard,' said he to me while fixing his black gaze on my visage as if he could plainly discern the shelves and goblets on the wall behind me, that my figure blocked from view. I tried to look away and evade his suggestion, thus returning my thoughts to the secret confines of my own, inner musings, but, to my consternation, I could not. '*Consequuntur actiones omni causa*,' quoth he to insist on knowing the cause of my inattention and evasion, but I, with a dismissive wave of the hand, decried the existence of any formidable cause for so feeble an effect. I could not look away, and still his gaze demanded to know wherefore I was thus distracted. Without meaning or wishing to, I acquiesced and spoke my thoughts to this dark robbed figure as if needing to make confession of my frequent descents into melancholy.

"'Oft I think of when last I saw my father. He was wont to call me to his side, to regale me, at the end of the day, of his itinerant journeys about the estates, his meetings with tenant farmers and town tradesmen, his musings over accounts and legal documents.

"'On such a day in Reigate Manor, we spoke of events no doubt far beyond the ken of a child of 7 years, events that would envelope my family in the rolling tides of history and the ebbs and flows of England's fortunes. He wanted me to know, to prepare me for events and happenstances from which he knew that he could not shield me.

"'The old King was sick and riddled with pain, spreading from the stinking sore on his leg to the whole of his once much praised body. He was tired of the endless battles between courtiers who tore at each other like cats, to claw their path to a position of favour before the old hunk of rotting flesh should succumb to the final agony. For years, had he held them at bay, seeming to favour one faction and then the other, so as to preclude either from total dominance and power. Now he wished only to die in peace, knowing that his son would not be split in twain, like the child of Solomon's tale, by the envious and ambitious rivals of power.

"'King Henry, however, was nursing another injury, not of his body, ravaged and rotting though it was, but of his manly countenance and princely pride. Six times did he take to bed a wife, and all but one, it seems did hurt him, mock him, betray church and state at once in their pride or lust. Two of them he had executed, their heads dispatched on Tower Green, and both of those unfortunate recreants had been of our blood, Howard women, cousins of my father, though as far from him in temperament as is a hawk from a nightingale. My grandfather, whose Norfolk lineage stretched back four hundred years, was already chap fallen from loss of the King's favour, and my father, who had wanted nothing more than to raise his family and write his lines, found himself the object of Edward Seymour's jealous calumny.

"'Seymour knew that the King would not last much longer, and that, in the hands of the guardian and protector of the boy who would succeed him, rested the unchecked power and pleasures of the realm. So did this Seymour set about to dispatch his only possible rivals for the guardianship. Who else but Norfolk and Surrey, father and son of royal, Plantagenet blood, whose family had been at the forefront of every battle to crush England's enemies and secure her crown?

"'Seymour, whose sister, Jane, had been the young prince's mother, enjoyed, thereby, kinship with England's heir. To counter this, my father changed the heraldry of his standard, and that of my grandfather of Norfolk, by superimposing thereupon the three lions rampant of Plantagenet – still the royal emblem of our sovereign lord. Upon this did the envious Seymour seize, and did at once protest to the King that Duke and Earl, of Howard blood, were traitors and usurpers. Thus swiftly did the King's armoured lancers steal into the dead of night to lay hold of my father and dispatch him, shackled like a brigand, to the Tower.

"'I never saw my father again. He was made to pay an onerous price for three golden lions rampant on a field of crimson, for imprudence, yes, but for treason, never.'

"Doctor Michel had not ceased to hold me with his piercing gaze, but had all the while said nothing. Now, without releasing his penetrating stare, he spoke, as if of something he could plainly see, among my thoughts:

"'...Strange how such seeming little things determine who shall live and who shall die? So you were orphaned for the name and pedigree of a family, for three golden lions, by three golden lions?'

"'I could not stop those evil men who spirited my father away that night. I would not stop them. I did not stop them, nor did I try to stop them...' I repeated as if it were the antiphon of a Litany of the Saints.

"I finally broke the lock of his gaze and, with all my strength, forbore to turn again my eyes to where I knew his own awaited. I looked only at the knotted oak table before me and said nothing. Thus sat I sullen for a long while, and all the talk around me had ceased. I raised my gaze and saw each eye fixed on my surely troubled face. I saw in each face a singular look, in each look a singular concern, a question unformed. When next I commenced my narrative, I spoke not only to Doctor Michel, but to all of them.

"'I will never forget the sound of knocking at the great oaken door of the keep: pounding, pounding like the paws of a great beast at the wooden barrier, a rhythmic drumming as if to wake the dead.' The room fell silent as I lowered my gaze to indicate that my tale was done.

"Gaudin was the first to speak. 'None could have foretold thy father's fate, nor could any man have saved him from his predestined end.'

"'My friend,' spake I in patient tone to tell that of which I was so certain. 'I knew he would die, knew it as if it had already happened, yet I cowered in fear at the sound of the knocking. I did nothing to change or forestall the course of events the ends of which were so certain.'

"After this, we all fell silent, and drank our maudlin draughts."

Chapter 4
We Assign Ourselves a Project

The shadows of evening come early to Paris this time of year. So, with the light rapidly fading in the garden courtyard of my pension-hotel on *rue de la Comet*, I gathered up my papers and my precious diary and prepared to take a walk in the chilly evening air before going over to Hank's for dinner. She had appointed herself my research assistant and had invited me over, ostensibly, to compare notes on Howard family history. I enjoyed watching her get excited over some small detail before turning around and levelling me with one of her teasing glances, when I had the temerity to disagree with her. I was following what was by now a familiar course, along the imperial bridge that led like a military column to the Napoleonic temple of *Les Invalids*. My thoughts, however, kept pulling me back to my work.

Although my diarist described such occurrences, as the one just related, with a certain amount of deliberation and detachment, Howard was an actor in the events he described and not just an observer. He was not adverse to examining and questioning his own motives and circumstances to a larger extent than he ever questioned the motives of others. Howard had escaped from turbulent events to a place where the rules about being at home were much more relaxed, but was he headed towards the rest of his life or away from all that remained of it? Do lives have direction, purpose and ends, or do they just plod along from moment to moment taking any one of several possible paths? If we are constantly repeating our past mistakes, is it possible to anticipate the future, just as we can revisit the past, and by a subtle change of course avoid seemingly inevitable consequences? If we were to have more than one chance to make life altering decisions, how likely is it that we would end up in the same place anyway?

These were questions that Howard had put into his journal on some cold and rainy winter night huddled around the meagre warmth of a candle's flame, tilting his book into the small circle of light around which complete and total darkness was pressing like an inky sea. He permitted himself these reflections in between his accounts of boisterous tavern trysts and long somnolent Latin lectures from threadbare friars who held classes in converted barns and out-buildings. Howard commented about how he and his fellow students would settle down on straw covered floors, trying to avoid stepping or sitting in the urine or fesses of the people and animals who had been there before.

When he was not writing about his friends or the buxom barmaids, or the clerical masters who lectured on rhetoric, philosophy, theology and Socratic logic, or the mysterious Doctor Michel who haunted the same drinking holes as did the students and their still youthful masters, he would reflect on why he was here. By "here", he did not mean just his own damp and dingy room, but this particular location in time for whatever larger purpose might later come to light. Howard seemed to enjoy these kinds of musings which, in some way, allowed him to make some sense out of the string of events that had gone before.

Hank's apartment was up three flights of stairs in an older building on Rue St Dominique. The hallway was dark with discoloured, greying walls of rough, uneven plaster. Her door (marked 3E) was heavy and equipped with a double tumbler lock. No one would get in there unless they were let in. When she opened for me, the passage was suddenly awash with light and colour from two lamps and an overhead fixture that dispelled the gloominess of the hallway. The walls, as well, were painted a cheerful peach colour, and there was a feeling of warmth that came from her innate ability to match her simple furnishings to the kinds of spaces she needed to fill. She handed me a glass of white wine, a *vin du paye* from the Loire, and shepherded me to the coach, where she had a manila folder stuffed with her Howard notes and bibliographical references.

"All right," she said, crossing her legs and flipping her hair out of her eyes, "here is what I've got:

"Henry Howard's grandfather was Thomas Howard, Duke of Norfolk and Earl Marshal of England, one of the most powerful figures in the court of Henry VIII and the uncle of both Anne Boleyn and Catherine Howard, the disgraced and beheaded queens. After Catherine Howard's execution, the Duke, her uncle, retired from court to look after his country estates, hoping that his removal from under the King's eye might enable him to avoid the full weight of the royal wrath. This left his eldest son, Henry Howard, the Earl of Surrey, responsible for looking after the family's interests at court."

"Oh yes, we know all about Surrey, the poet."

"And I've checked out the account from the journal, of how the Earl of Surrey fell out of the royal favour, for having decided to take on the Seymours. According to my notes, he was sentenced to death on January 13, 1547 and beheaded on Tower Green six days later. His wife and children became wards of the crown and were given over to the widow of the King's bastard son, a kindly young woman who was also their Aunt Mary (Howard). Aunt Mary was charged with their financial security and the further education of the children. The younger boy, Henry, was seven years old, at the time."

"Yes, I forgot to tell you about the Henry Fitzroy and Mary Howard branch of the family tree."

Hank ignored me and just kept talking. "The Duke, the grandfather, was finally sentenced to follow his son to the chopping block, but the King died first, and the old man was left, by the Seymours, to rot in the Tower.

"The family remained in semi-disgrace (suspected of latent Catholic sympathies) during the brief reign of King Henry's only surviving son. So it was that Henry Howard was schooled by a hand-picked tutor, for the next six years, under the watchful eye of his de Vere mother and Howard aunt, until in July of 1553, Mary Tudor became Queen. She promptly set about rewarding those previously out of favour and sending to the block those who had prospered under her Protestant brother and his guardians."

"So the Howards were restored to favour by Queen Mary for their so-called Catholic leanings?"

"One of her first acts, as Queen, was to order the release of the old Duke of Norfolk, from the Tower. What's more, she took a particular interest in the education of young Henry and eventually arranged to have him travel to Paris to attend the University there. She had a need, so she said, for courtiers with the right kind of education, and also with knowledge of the ways of the world. She assured young Howard that his family would be well cared for in his absence, and that a place in court would await him, upon his return."

"Yes, it seemed that the tide of events was to be kinder to the younger Henry Howard than it had been to the elder. That would account for all of those journal entries referring to how his father had died and actually expressing anxiety, even guilt, about his own good fortune.

"In a sense, it was like being rewarded for not saving his father from certain death. It seemed to him that the brave often go to the block and those who stand by and do nothing are rewarded and praised for their inaction. Was he, in fact, to profit from his father's death? Did he somehow want his father to die so that he could have all of these good things?"

"Don't get carried away, Michael," said Hank with one of those looks that are usually able to bring me back to a more detached and scholarly approach to the available evidence. "Remember, this is Henry Howard we're talking about, not Sigmund Freud!"

"I still think that these questions haunted young Howard and chased him across the channel and all the way from Calais to Paris. He had a real case of hero worship for is father. He talks about having carefully stowed in the recesses of his travel bag, some volumes of his father's poetry, little morsels of a kind of immortality, the only part of the elder Henry Howard that the headsman was not able to take away. He writes about dreaming of executions and murders and waking up in a sweat, not wondering if he himself were dead but asking why he had been left alive at such a cost. I guess I keep thinking of his finding himself in a strange city, in another country, where he knew more Latin for the classroom than French for ordering a meal in a tavern. He describes himself as someone tossed by an absurd and wayward destiny into a place where he had to act out what he was evidently meant to do, to become the man he was somehow meant to be."

Although Hank didn't appear to completely buy it, I was beginning to get a picture of this young man who had left me his words from four and a half centuries ago and who seemed to be coming alive again for me from these ancient and crumbling pages. I experienced a strange empathy for him, despite the differences of time and circumstance. I wanted to come to grips with his situation and try to understand how an adolescent, orphaned and alone in a city far from his home, managed his grudge against capricious circumstances and an overwhelming sense of - what was it – guilt, regret, anger? I reached out, with both my hands to hold Hank's attention long enough to get her to understand.

"Look. This was a kid who was confronting, in his own way, what we would nowadays call his personal 'ghosts'. I want to try to understand how he must have thought and felt about what he'd been through. Did he continue to feel his father's absence deeply, or did he resent the man for not being there when he needed him? Did it seem to Howard that his father had left him, so to speak, in the lurch, and did he hate himself for feeling that way? I have to find the words (his words) that will let me inside his head."

"...and you also have to keep enough objectivity about his words to be able to read what he meant to say or leave unsaid, to listen for his voice and not to drown it out with your own."

I shook my head, as if I were trying to wake myself up. There was Hank, sitting next to me with that bemused smile that was part scolding and part deep understanding, as if she could see deeply into the recesses of my innermost thoughts. She looked at me, her blue eyes repeatedly glancing in playful jealousy at the little book that had become an extension of my arm and hand. She moved to touch the book with her finger tips only to make me pull it away reflexively, so that she could give me that offended look that she knew I found irresistible.

"Listen," I said, "I need you to take a page of this to your friend at the *Prefecture* for an analysis of the handwriting. I need to establish, for sure, that Henry Howard actually wrote these pages. I have to be certain that this is genuine!"

Hank picked up on the fact that I had emphasized the word, "friend," a little more than I had to, and she nodded, while giving me a self-satisfied smile. "OK," she said. "What are you going to compare it against? You don't suppose that Henry Howard has a parking ticket on the municipal police data base anywhere?"

"Here," I said, reaching into the left breast pocket of my jacket. I pulled out a folded piece of paper, one of the photocopies I had taken in London, of the pages from Howard's 1583 *'Poison of Supposed Prophecies'* manuscript. 'This is from a private Howard family collection. We know this was written by Henry Howard about 28 years after the time of this journal. A handwriting specialist should be able to establish if this (and I pulled a single folded sheet from between two pages of the journal) was penned by the same person."

"Quite the little detective," teased Hank with her beguiling playfulness that did not quite mask her own excitement about the venture. "I can take this to Jean-Paul first thing tomorrow morning, or tonight, if you prefer."

"Tomorrow is quite soon enough," I said, not trying to hide my annoyance. This pleased her, and she smiled at me with the magnanimous forgiveness of one who knew she had won this round. I wondered if we could ever stop sparring long enough to tell each other how we really felt. Why is it that she can always make me feel like a stammering adolescent, when I'm around her? The feeling, I confess, is not at all unpleasant, but why does she have to enjoy it so much?

Hank saw that she was pushing me just about as far as I wanted to go, so she brought us back to the subject of the pages. "Are you prepared for the let down, if it turns out that Henry Howard did not write this journal?"

"It's still a great story," I said, feeling suddenly crest fallen at the possibility that, I confess, I hadn't seriously considered yet. I must have looked as deflated as I felt, for Hank tilted her head to one side, without a trace of her playful derision, and started to stroke the hand that held the book.

"This means a lot to you, doesn't it?" she asked with uncharacteristic tenderness.

"If it IS genuine, it could be a very important piece of evidence!"

"It still doesn't prove that he was Shakespeare," said Hank, trying to help me to rein in my expectations.

"No, it doesn't," I admitted. I was about to add a "but", when I lost my train of thought and just sat there thinking about what we had just said.

Chapter 5
Howard's Story Begins

Since the 12th century, the University of Paris had been administratively divided into four "nations": the French, the Normans, the Picards and the English, but at least 200 years before Howard got there, the name of the "English" nation was changed to the "Allemande" or "Germanic" nation, because of hard feelings over the 100 Years' War. As housing accommodations were always a problem in Paris, living arrangements had been made for Howard at the *Collège du Cardinal Lemoine* on *rue St. Victor*, a ramshackle residence named for the 14th Century Papal legate who had been sent to Paris to make peace between the English and the French.

So it was that the seventeen year old Henry Howard, his stuffed satchel slung over one shoulder, slouched through the low front door of what looked like a boarding house to be confronted by a broad backed, middle aged matron who stood blocking the entrance hall. She was holding a broom, the staff of her authority, with both hands: her left hand high on the handle and her right down close to the bristles, as if it were a musket, ready to be levelled at the unwary traveller who dared cross her threshold. The self-appointed sentry bellowed her challenge in the direction of the open door. "*Qui êtes vous, jeune homme? Qu'est que vous voulez ici, enfant vagabond!*"

Frightened and tired after his long coach ride, the last leg of which had taken him from Beauvais, via overnight bumpy roads squeezed between two bulging sacks of mail, Howard could not make his mouth form the few polite French words he had learned. Instead, he fell into a sitting position, quickly pulling his satchel around to cushion his aching behind, and, looking up plaintively from the ground, he said in halting Latin:

"*Sum discipulus Terrae Anglorum in universitate Lutetiae*" ("I am an English student at the University of Paris.")

The woman, unimpressed by Howard's learning, hurled the broom to the floor, the better to menace the boy with her red knuckled fists that seemed the size of cannonballs from Howard's position on the floor. "I don't speak your piggish student Latin, learned vagabond!" said the old lady, having summoned all her dignity to say so. "Here we speak like common folk, the vulgate you call us, while you student brats and your clerical masters too, drink and carouse and break windows all night, then piss in the alleys and hallways before falling asleep in your drunken stupors!" She raised herself to her full height of indignation before the cowering boy, then turned, as if ashamed of her own leniency and mumbled, "You might as well come in out of the cold. You look half-starved and too tired to run. You're not good for any damage to my humble house tonight, and I can't let you shiver and starve in the street, although by God that's what I have half a mind to do."

Howard jumped to his feet and scrambled inside before the old matron changed her mind. He managed to mumble "*Merci*" in the old lady's general direction, just enough French to assuage her temper and calm the situation down.

Once the door was closed behind him, the broad shouldered landlady began to speak to her latest tenant as if the previous conversation had been about someone else. "You could use some hot soup and dark bread and a tankard of red wine to get your strength back, young man. – What did you say your name was?"

"*Je m'appele Henry Howard*," he said, still terrified of forgetting his French and re-igniting the woman's wrath.

"Very well, *Henri* Howard," the old woman said in a surprisingly soothing voice, speaking slowly (for her) and making sure to enunciate careful for his benefit. "We have several foreign students in residence here, but I'm putting you in with a Breton lad, named Gaston Gaudin. He'll help you improve your French, so you don't starve to death in this city," she added, with some of the old contempt back in her voice. "We have rules here about when you can come in at night and whom you can bring in with you." She had stepped away from the door to shake her finger close to his panic stricken face. "You'd better remember them, if you don't want to end up sleeping in a barn or between two grave markers in a church yard!"

Howard thanked her for the food, the drink and the advice. He turned his attention to his meal, which he wolfed down as if someone were about to take it away. By the time he was finished, he felt warm and peaceful and almost too tired to keep his eyes open. Promising to be quiet as the dead and to abide by all of the establishment's rules, he excused himself and climbed the stairs to his new room.

Gaudin, it turned out, was a year older than Howard, a head taller and very much the expert on where to go in the city, where the best (and least expensive) restaurants and taverns were and whose lectures were the most sought after or the most boring. Their conversations freely flowed from Latin to English to French, seemingly without impediment on either side to understand or to respond. They hit it off instantly, or almost instantly, since Gaudin was asleep and snoring loudly when Howard entered their shared room, neither of which circumstances bothered Howard who could have slept through the siege of Troy, at that point. The next morning, however, Gaudin decided to take the younger Howard under his wing and introduce him to his own circle of friends and fellow students.

Chapter 6
The Circle of Friends

Journal Entry 22 May, 1557

"That's when things started to look up for me and when I began to feel that this new life had superseded the memories and horrors that had come before. My days were filled with new experiences, new learning, new friends and always something in the magnificent city to see. The nights, too, now opened new possibilities for expanding my knowledge and experience of the pleasures, as well as the perils, of my new life. Back in rural Sussex, I could never have imagined that these kinds of experiences were there for the taking, but now the fellowship, the wine and the plump tavern girls were at my beck and command, and command them I did.

"Even Madame Beber, the Amazon innkeeper whose breath, that first night, had visited both the smell of garlic and the fear of God upon me, turned out to be more bellow than blow. More often than not, she would help my older, more "worldly" room mate guide me, in my inebriated state, up the twisted stairs, around which the hall seemed to be spinning under the influence of the ale that I, a neophyte drinker, had consumed that night. In my stupor, I noticed solicitude, even maternal tenderness in the old lady's face.

"'This is Claude Dormoy' said Gaudin with a magnanimous wave of his hand in the direction of a morose looking young man sitting hunched over a pewter tankard of ale into which the youth was staring, as if in meditation.

We were assembled in Gaudin's favourite tavern, next to the stables which belonged to the *curé* of *Sainte-Geneviève*, directly across from the Faculty of Law. We had come to wash from our throats the feeling of dry dust which was all that remained of an afternoon reading from the *Codex Juris Canonici* by the distinguished Father Eusebius Berdelini, O.F.M., of the Law Faculty. This was one of the requirements in the scope of our course in rhetoric, to introduce us to the stylistic peculiarities of ecclesiastical Latin. As the only known antidote to Father Eusebius was a tankard of ale from Picardy, we had decided to take the cure at the *Ecurie*, as the tavern was called, where a large student population had also gathered, to drown the memory of the venerable Franciscan's voice with the raucous laughter of Marie Blanchard, the *Ecurie's* ebullient innkeeper.

"The public room, at the *Ecurie*, was only accessible by descending a narrow, winding staircase, at the bottom of which stretched a long and vaulted cave of exposed beams and mortared stones. I had arranged to meet Gaudin there, and the latter wasted no time introducing me to what he referred to as his 'inner circle' of friends.

"The older students, it seemed, had had a head start on Father Eusebius' latest batch of initiates, having already partaken of several rounds of reddish amber ale from the Abbey of St Linus, near Lille. The noise in the place was deafening. Much of the ruckus centred around the bar stool of the morose looking young man whom Gaudin was attempting to present to me, in between the rounds of riotous laughter.

"'Dormoy, this is the Worthy Henry Howard, from England. You two have a lot in common,' jeered Gaudin, to the delight of the small crowd that was pressing closer to the bar stool where Dormoy sat, transfixed by the contents of his tankard. 'He can't speak French worth a damn, either.' Gaudin delivered his punch line in a 'stage whisper,' while looking all around him for approval. At his queue, half the room, it seemed, roared its approval with guffaws, whistles and catcalls, as everyone enjoyed another laugh at the hapless Dormoy's expense.

"For his part, Dormoy, still pretending that his ale was more captivating than the gaggle of youths all around him, raised his dark dog-like eyes to my face, offered one hand and signalled with the other to a barmaid, pointing first to his tankard and then to me, his new friend. 'I come from Cavaillon, in Provence,' said Dormoy in a thickly Italianate Latin, by way of explaining what all the commotion was about. 'We speak *Provençal* down there,' he added, 'and those of us who do speak French, have, so they tell me, a very heavy accent.'

"'Hey Dormoy' called a voice from the crowd, 'Where is your DOG?' ('*Ou est votre CHIEN?*').

"Dormoy, no longer ignoring them in his ale, took the bait. '*Je n'est pas de CHIANG!*' ('I don't have a dog!').

"This provoked another round of laughter and a chorus of voices repeating: '*CHIANG ... CHIANG ... CHIANG!* ' followed by a refrain of hoots and whistles.

"'You see what I mean?' asked Dormoy, laughing quietly as his own mispronunciation.

"Now Gaudin, the self-appointed master of the revels, raised his hands in a mock-magnanimous gesture, as if to say that he, for one, was above all of this sophomoric banter. He motioned to Dormoy and me to join him at a more distant table, away from the boisterous multitudes, the better to pursue the more serious business of getting drunk and meeting that barmaid with the magnificent breasts.

"'I inspected the worry lines and the furrowed brow on the hang-dog face of my newest acquaintance. 'Don't give them the satisfaction of taking their mockery thus to heart.'

"'Oh, he's not worried about them!' Gaudin interrupted, his finger high in the air, as he appraised the situation from his all-knowing vantage point. 'Our Dormoy, you see, has just returned from burying his mother in Cavaillon. Plague, it was, that took her with deadly swiftness. I think he's still angry with God about it.'

"'Dormay looked away, the wound being too fresh for him to trust a reply to words. He would have gotten up to leave them, at this point, except that his escape was blocked by a remarkably beautiful young waitress who was angling toward their table, deftly juggling five tankards of ale.

"'*Haec puella est pulcherima in urbe!* '('This one's the prettiest girl in the city!'), proclaimed Gaudin in conspiratorial Latin, punching me lightly on the shoulder. He nodded with emphasis at the red haired beauty who, at that moment, was bending to place one of the brimming tankards before me. Her seemingly unconscious action drew my uninitiated eyes to the low laced bodice, pulled tight to the point of bursting over her ample bosom.

"She looked at me, then at the smirking Gaudin. Turning back to me she said, nodding disdainfully at the master of ceremonies: '*Hic puer canis salus est!*' ('This boy is a filthy cur!').

"Both Dormoy and I roared with laughter, as the deflated master shrunk on his stool. Quickly, Gaudin recovered his composure and started to laugh, as well.

"'I thought you said that we can talk about these barmaids in Latin because they won't have any idea about what we are saying,' I commented, when I finally caught my breath.

"'I told you'" answered Gaudin. 'This one is different. She's heard all of the "*puella*" lines that have ever been thought of, and she has some stock come-back phrases of her own, as well. You might call it self-defense Latin.' The three of us laughed again, in genuine admiration of this clever and comely girl.

"While the three of us continued to enjoy our own wit, the bar maid had moved on to a nearby table to serve up a tankard to a heavy set young man with an unruly mass of dark, curly hair and thick bushy eyebrows, which gave him the appearance of having an unusually large head. The stocky youth not only accepted his ale but was deep in conversation with the young serving wench. I could tell immediate from the animated manner with which the curly haired fellow was gesturing and slicing the air with his index finger that the boy was Italian.

"This provided more intelligence about the bar maid, based on the evident fact that there was no language barrier between him and the girl. Dormoy noted, as well, that the girl was being as pleasant to this Italian as she had been contemptuous toward Gaudin. For his part, Gaudin merely tipped back his stool so that his feet were elevated and his back was wedged against the stone wall. He smiled knowingly and, once the girl had moved on, he called in a loud and commanding voice: 'Giambelli, come over here and tell us all about the mysteries of women.'

"The Italian youth nodded acknowledgement and, theatrically easing back his stool by pushing the table in front of him, rose and sauntered over to us three companions with an air of complete self-assurance. Dormoy went over to a nearby table and returned with a stool which he proffered the Italian. Giambelli bowed his acceptance, sat down and brought his tankard of ale to rest in formation with the other three. Gaudin launched his back from the wall, bringing the front legs of his stool back down to the floor. Leaning across the table, he pointed at me and said: 'Bernardo Giambelli, I present the Worthy Henry Howard, from England. Of course, you know Claude Dormoy, the Provençal who speaks French like a Spanish cow.'

"Gaudin smiled to himself again as he volunteered some more of his sardonic advice. 'Don't call him "Giambelli" in front of his countrymen, though. Bernardo, here, comes from Portecorvo, where his schoolmates used to refer to him as "Testagrossa". So, to make him feel more at home, we mostly call him "Father Testagrossa." Everyone laughed at Gaudin's latest witticism, even Giambelli, who bowed to the company, as if he had just been offered a title of particular honour.

"'Why FATHER Testagrossa?' In my puzzlement, I was oblivious to the general approval being given to Gaudin as Master of Revels.

"'Because,' answered the Italian, 'unlike the rest of this profane gathering, I intend to go on to the priesthood and plumb the depths of theology, as did my ancient countryman, *Tommaso d'Aquino*.'

"'Yes,' added Gaudin. 'And in two years, he'll become a sub-deacon. Then they'll have to tie his big head in a knot, because he won't be using it any more.'

"'Much to the loss of that barmaid who evidently vastly prefers Testagrossa's company to yours,' added Dormoy, relishing a chance to strike a retaliatory blow. This merited another round of laughter and ale.

"Whether he was speaking Latin or French, Testagrossa's pronunciation was as full and rounded as his hand gestures, and he rolled his 'r's in the same manner as Dormoy – not at all in the Parisian fashion.

"'So what's your secret for charming the girls' I asked, still thinking of the buxom waitress.

"'Oh, you mean Caterina!' said Testagrossa, raising his hands in the air as if he were about to give a blessing. 'Well, these pigs treat her like a kitchen slut, but I treat her like a *Bella Signorina*,' which I assure you she is,' concluded the young Italian with a flourish, his large head sitting straight upon his shoulders and his jaw fixed and firm as a marble statue, his aquiline nose slightly elevated like a bust of Lorenzo the Magnificent. 'A woman,' he continued, 'is a vessel of beauty and grace, a work of perfection by means of which we glimpse the magnificence of God Himself.'

"'I think Howard, here, got a good glimpse of Caterina's magnificence a moment ago,' observed Dormoy, glancing over at Gaudin, who had not gotten anything memorable from the aforementioned experience.

"We would have continued to wax rhapsodic about Caterina's virtues and attributes had we not been distracted by a boisterous explosion of singing starting from the far end of the room nearest the staircase. '*Je vous salut, Marie*,' rang the mock prayerful voices, greeting first the skirts and then the whole form of the inn keeper, Marie Blanchard, who had just come from the kitchen with hot trays of food to spread before the multitudes to stave off drunkenness and vomiting in her respectable establishment. Marie and a heavy set man with a sauce stained apron and a vacant expression on his face struggled to hoist a huge copper cauldron onto a long table at the front of the vaulted cave. The steaming pot vented the intoxicating fragrance of a savoury mutton stew which Caterina and the portly kitchen menial began to ladle into wooden bowls while passing the bowls to the waiting hands of the famished boys. Each recipient then pulled a handful of bread from one of the loaves that were piled on an adjacent platter and used his bread to soak up the stew and convey the bowl's contents to his mouth.

"Gaudin, Dormoy, Testagrossa and I found a table off to one side, where we could enjoy our free meal away from the clamouring throngs. We ate as if this were the first meal we had had and the last good meal we were likely to get for several days. Dormoy was grateful that Gaudin talked less so that he could eat more. The combination of food, noise and the free flow of ale added to the rising tide of good spirits and camaraderie."

Chapter 7
My First Encounters
with City Life

Journal Entry Continues

"**W**ith our stomachs full and spirits high, we four friends sauntered out into the night heading down the *Montaigne Sainte-Geneviève* in the general direction of the river and the older students' more familiar haunts. Dusk had already begun to envelop the streets and alleys and paint the city in drab and fading colours. We were urinating in a near-by alley and singing a ballad about dying for love, when Gaudin spotted the rapid movement of shadows diving for cover at the opposite end of the alley. Still singing at the top of his voice, so as not to let on that he was alert to the presence of the intruders, he nodded to the rest of us to reverse course and head back to the street entrance. Brave with drink, we were not as yet stupid enough to be fearless, and we agreed to follow the main streets where there would be the added security of activity and witnesses.

"We knew, of course, that street gangs seldom targeted students because they were perennially penniless, threadbare and seldom in possession of anything worth stealing. Students also tended to travel in company, and street thugs were known to steer clear of anything resembling a fair fight, except when gang wars pitted one side against the other and all restraint was forgotten in the barrage of tree branches, stones and blacksmith's anvils. Almost at a given signal, on those nights when it seemed like armies were rising like rats out of the sewers, people would close their doors, shutter their windows and snuff out all of their candles to wait out the storm.

"This, however, was not such a night. As we wound past rolling wagons pushing through the *rue des Ecoles*, we saw men engaged in unloading ponderous wheels of cheese and racks of smoked meats, bolts of cloth and lengths of tanned leather ready to be cut and sown into purses, shoes and saddle bags. The bustle spilled over into the wide length of the St Germain, where men were hammering make-shift booths and stands into place and erecting rickety tents with sticks and blankets, under which to secure their goods.

"All this frenetic activity was a hasty preparation for the *Saint Germain* Fair, which would spring to life with the next day's dawning and envelop the entire Left Bank in its festive frenzy. The four of us took a side street past the old church of *Saint-Séverin*, in the direction of a particularly run-down looking tavern, when, all at once, the church bells pealed out the evening *Angelus*. Hands immediately released hammers, bolts of cloth and tent poles to make the sign of the cross. One of a pair of nearby nuns was heard mumbling the words: "*Angelus Domini nuntiavit Mariae*", to which the other responded: "*Et concepit de Spiritu Sancto*," and in the time it took to say three "*Ave's*" all hands had returned to their labours.

"Another class of workers chose this moment to move into position for their nightly duties. Groups of women, dressed in bright colours adorned with ruffs and silk stitching, made dance-like movements in brightly beaded shoes with elevated leathered heels. On cue, the women took up pre-ordained positions on the steps leading up to the old church. Clearly, they had not come to pray, as they gathered their skirts about them and raised them sufficiently to display their high heeled shoes and silk hose. That night, seven of them sat evenly distributed in a three dimensional pattern up and down the church steps, striking casual poses and shaking back their heads to allow their long tresses of hair to fly loose and cascade like silk waterfalls over their pink shoulders and into the cleft between out-stretched breasts.

"'Holy Mother of God...' I exclaimed, having caught sight of one particular raven haired beauty, still evidently uncomfortably new at this, whose huge eyes were deep blue pools of warm and glistening liquid. She shifted her position ever so slightly, and I thought I could hear the stiff cloth of the crenulated shift that assuredly lay beneath her skirt as it rubbed against her thigh like a tender twig.

"'Close your mouth, Howard,' said Dormoy looking genuinely embarrassed at my apparent naivety.

"'Yes,' said Gaudin. 'She might think you're having an epileptic fit. She'll take you to one of their doctors who specialize in syphilis and epilepsy, two common ailments among whores.'

"'As usual, our model for sensitivity and respect,' commented Testagrossa putting a fatherly hand on my shoulder. 'One must respect women as the very pinnacle of God's creation. On the other hand,' the young Italian added with a self-deprecating shrug, 'One cannot help but admire women as the very pinnacle of Nature's handiwork! Therein lies the dilemma of the human condition.'

"'Oh shut up, you prig!' said Gaudin, who was getting increasing irritated with his philosophical friend. 'That's the most fat-headed remark I have ever heard. You persist in confusing love with lust, which is a simple human vice, in which many of us engage daily without so much as a second thought about the nobility of human nature or the eternal destiny of man,' pronounced Gaudin, his right hand raised in a rhetorical gesture.

"'Do you deny the eternal destiny of man?' asked Testagrossa, his own right hand cutting through the air opposite Gaudin's.

"'By no means,' added the leader of revels, 'but why must it interfere with my pleasure?'

"While my two friends were thus engaged in a truly eternal debate, the workers whose preparations for the morning market were now complete had decided to reward themselves for their evening's labours by sampling the church step wares. They sauntered up alone and strolled away in couples with an ease and grace that one would truly expect of hereditary nobility, while we observers were left with our words.

"This gave Dormoy a new sense of purpose. 'I think,' he postulated with the smoothness of a southerner, 'that it is time to initiate our young friend into the mysteries and the pleasures of the night.'

"'With a prostitute?' asked Testagrossa in genuine indignation.

"'What's the difference?' asked Gaudin with a cavalier disregard for his friend's sensitivity. 'They're all sisters under their shifts, you know,' he added, strutting a few steps, like a rooster.

"'It should be one he fancies,' counselled Dormoy. 'The first time should be special.'

"'Every time is special for me,' said Gaudin, still perfecting the rooster movement with his neck.

"I ignored them all and just stepped out, slowly and tentatively, in the direction of the dark haired girl. I caught her eye and she turned toward me so that I could have a full frontal view of her low bodice framed with her silky, shining hair, darker than the night sky. I drew in my breath. I could feel myself shaking and I was sure that I was about to lose my courage, turn and run, but the girl boldly fixed her gaze, those enormous pools of blue luminosity, on me. Like a force greater than the pounding surf and inexorable tides, her eyes drew me into the sphere of her power and the deft practice of her art.

"My friends broke off their extended debate on the nature and destiny of man to notice that one man, at least, had already taken matters into his own trembling hands. They felt as if they were watching someone in a dream, walking through a door without any knowledge of what he might find on the other side. They were both happy and afraid for me, and not one of them thought to call out any words of banter or of advice. I was beyond their sphere, well past the need for anyone's advice.

"They were so taken up with my chosen path that they failed to notice the return of the shadows in the recesses of the nearby booths. Suddenly and inexplicably, the workers all disappeared under their stalls and the girls abruptly broke their poses and fled into three of the adjacent alleys, amid the crinkling of skirt against shifts. My dark beauty was the last to leave, with a momentary, side-long glance in my direction, permitting her to mouth the words, 'Ask for *Julie*.' Before my friends and I knew what was happening, eight dark and emaciated youths emerged from the streets behind them.

"Their clothes were rags and their hands and faces were black with soot and street dust, but their eyes were luminous and predatory like wolves. Five of them were holding make-shift clubs, torn from the large hanging branches of trees, and the others brandished fists that shone by the light of a near-by torch with the lurid red of bloody scabs and old scars. The four of us stood like rooted trees, exposed to the elements, when we realized that the eight youths were ignoring us. Instead, the predators were circling like a pack toward four small figures who had just had the misfortune to emerge from one of the three alleys into which the prostitutes had fled just moments before.

"The strangers' clothing was dark, so it was difficult to distinguish them at first. There was a man, a woman and two children, girls, the youngest of which could not have been older than seven years. The man wore a plain jerkin, tied, at the waist, with a broad belt over loose fitting trousers and high boots. There was neither lace collar no any mark of contrast about his dress, and on his head, he wore a tall hat that looked like a tower with a broad rim about the bottom. The woman was equally plain in her attire, without the slightest hint of colour or ornament, and her hair was completely hidden beneath a tight fitting white bonnet tied neatly beneath her chin. As the children, too, were bonneted, without a single, playful hair in sight, in dresses as devoid of colour as that of their mother, we concluded that this must be a family of Huguenots who had just emerged from an evening prayer service in the home of one of their co-religionists.

"Slowly, the eight youths encircled the hapless family of four moving ever closer and hissing 'heretics, heretics' through uneven, yellow and clenched teeth. The parents instinctively formed a kind of human barrier between the manoeuvring attackers and the children, mother and father each on one side, arms joined and bound around the little ones.

"A particularly vigilant street vendor must have given a thought to the protection of his wares and run off to find one of the mounted companies of the *Duc de Guise*, who were currently enforcing the peace in the city. For presently, a troop of five armoured horsemen entered the square and took up position at the far end. As soon as they realized that only a Huguenot family and not the vendors' stalls were in any jeopardy, they hung back, with exchanged sniggers and some relief, to watch the spectacle.

"A tall youth, who occupied the forward juncture point of two columns of ruffians, launched himself at the tight family formation, delivering a blow to the father's kidney causing him to fold and collapse in pain. A second youth then moved in to separate the other three, roughly pushing the smallest child aside. She cried out as her elbow made contact with a cobble stone, before she skidded to a halt, face down in the street. Two other youths now grabbed the mother and older daughter from behind and held them while the leader made for the mother's skirts and taunted her about what he intended to do.

"All of a sudden, I heard a cry like the roar of an enraged animal and saw my philosophical friend, Testagrossa, lurch at the assailants closest to the women, his fists clenched and his head lowered into a battering ram. He struck the lead youth from behind, sending him flailing to the ground on all fours. Surprised and momentarily confused by the assault on their leader, the two youths behind them released the women's arms and regrouped with two others who had come around to assist.

"'*Courez*' ('Run!'), Testagrossa shouted at the released captives. The mother darted to where her youngest lay and, grasping her firmly by the hand, moved away, one daughter trailing from each hand.

"By now, the leader was back on his feet and organising a counter attack. Testagrossa and the father stood back to back and positioned themselves between the youths and the fleeing women. Suddenly, the Italian student and the father were flanked by Dormoy and me. I answered my friend's questioning eyes through clenched teeth: 'I hate bullies!'

"The assailants, now faced with a new enemy, were in need of fresh tactics. One of the youths, who had let go his hold on the women, pick up a loose cobble stone and prepared to throw it at Testagrossa's large head. As the ruffian's torso pivoted and his right hand moved behind his ear, some one hit him from behind at the knees. He was lifted into the air, his legs flying in front of him as he fell to the ground in a heap. His attacker, of course, was Gaudin, who grinned at us to indicate that the tide of this battle had clearly turned.

"Before there could be another round, however, the armoured horsemen moved into place between the two camps and turned their horses' flanks against us black robbed students. One soldier raised a pike and struck Testagrossa on the side of his head, sending him reeling to the ground. Another menaced Dormoy with his drawn sword and would have struck the unarmed youth had the group not fallen back and taken cover behind a nearby wagon. The troop leader addressed us from a-top his stamping smoking charger, in words that I render in my journal which, although in English, convey, more or less, the tone and ferocity :

"'Back to your scholarly shit holes, you drunken Latins,' he thundered, his drawn sword punctuating the air for emphasis. 'See to it that you don't harass honest townies out for a little fun with some of our local heretics.'

"Testagrossa, who had not made it to the wagon, rose slowly from the street where he had fallen, his head throbbing and his chest heaving with the effort. 'Tell the *Duc de Guise*', he snarled, blinking up at the Captain of the troop, 'that his King does not authorise him to make war on women and children.'

"The guard captain was poised to strike him again, this time with the hilt of his sword, when I emerged from behind the wagon and began to pull my friend toward our protective cover. I looked up at the armed horseman and declared with a '*sang-froid*' that I certainly did not feel: 'You have no authority over us. Only our provosts can meet out discipline, if warranted.'

"The captain sneered with irritation but pulled back his horse issuing a final command: 'Get you home to your rats' nests before I send you to your provost as stew meat!' The troop then turned their horses and moved away, the gang of youths having long since fled into the night.

"We sat for a while, huddled together on the ground, the four of us and the embattled Huguenot father. We breathed a sigh of relief and then realized in how much pain we were. The Huguenot father turned to us and lowering his head said: 'I cannot begin to thank you for saving my family from those ruffians, but why did you choose to help us, at your own peril?'

"Testagrossa, as usual, found the right words, as he had for a waitress and a prostitute that night. 'Did not our Lord tell of a man beaten by brigands and left for dead only to be saved by an outcast of another faith? What else could we do?'

"There was silence among the five of us then, as we rose, dusted off our clothing and tried our unsteady feet. Blood was seeping through the Huguenot's jerkin, and Testagrossa warned him not to go to a physician. 'They are butchers, all of them. They'll bleed you and do as much harm as your attackers.' He thought for a moment and then took the Huguenot by the arm. 'Take your family and go to the Abbey of *Sainte-Geneviève*. Ask for

Brother Anselm. He's a strange little man, but no one knows more about medicines and healing herbs than he does. They say he has read Hippocrates in the original Greek and that he reads Hebrew and Arabic, as well, to unlock the secrets and mysteries of Eastern medicine. He says that our modern doctors are barbarians compared to the ancients.'

"The father was still very unsteady on his feet. He looked up at his benefactor, a child-like expression overcoming the pain reflected on his face, '...but won't they turn us away as heretics and enemies of their faith?' he asked uncertainly.

"'St. Benedict gave them a strict rule of hospitality. They can't turn the needy from their gates, even if they are murderers. Besides, all you have to do is tell the brother gatekeeper that Bernardo Giambelli sent you and that you want to see Brother Anselm. He'll show you right in and take you to the herb garden. They all know me there, because of all the hours I pass in their library.' The young Huguenot was near to weeping, by now, with exhaustion and gratitude. 'Make sure he sees your little girl,' added Testagrossa after further consideration. 'She's received some pretty nasty cuts, and Anselm has a poultice that will prevent puss and swelling.' The young man nodded his gratitude, once again, and moved into the adjacent alley to re-join his family.

"The four us looked at each other and began to laugh at such a sorry and dishevelled company. Gaudin put his arm around Testagrossa and couldn't stop laughing. 'You're a disgrace, Father Testagrossa and I'm proud of you.'

"'We're all proud to call you our brother and our friend,' I added, smiling at Testagrossa's large unruly head and his torn black robe.

"'I'm tired,' said the young Italian, 'and I have to get some sleep if I'm going to hear mass tomorrow before we go to the fair.'

"After making arrangements to meet at *St. Séverin* at 9:00 am the next morning, we went our separate ways: Gaudin and I to the *rue St. Victor* to be cleaned, scolded and fussed over by our land lady, Mme. Beber, while Dormoy and Testagrossa headed back up the *Montaigne Sainte-Geneviève* to the *Ecurie* to be tended by Marie Blanchard, and the lovely Caterina."

Chapter 8
A Life Changing Event

Journal Entry 23 May, 1558

"**D**ormoy was the first to arrive at the square in front of *Saint-Séverin*. He was sporting a freshly washed cut over his right eye, and he was sure that this badge of combat earned him the unspoken respect of every street urchin and any other possible source of annoyance with which he might come into contact on his way to the appointed meeting place. There were no classes today, so the traditional, black academic robes were cast aside in favour of more casual jerkins, leggings and boots, although the colour and cut of Dormoy's clothes gave away his Provençal origins as surely as the twang of his French.

"Even after having spent three years in the northern capital, Dormoy was still awed by the spectacular transformation of the ordinarily drab streets and alleys of Paris when the *St Germain* Fair was in full flower. Each overhanging balcony shot out sprays of garish colour, in the form of pennants rippling in the wind from their balustrades. The streets were clogged with booths and stands and stationary, horseless wagons, displaying huge cuts of meat (beef, venison, wild boar) hanging on steel hooks, big enough to have dealt the fatal blow to the yet living animals. Everywhere there were cheeses, fruits and vegetables and small tables with bottles of home squeezed olive oil and berry flavoured vinegar. From one end of the St Germain to the other, the main boulevard and every side street was thick with moving, seething, serpentine humanity in a motley variety of colours and styles from all over France, Picardy, Navarre,

Luxembourg and the Low Countries. There were farmers, bakers and purveyors of medicines guaranteed to cure snake bites and syphilis sores. One could see jugglers, acrobats, fire eaters, musicians and dancers in exotic, foreign looking costumes. There were sections of the main boulevard marked off for members of specific guilds (such as the tanners, the tinkers and the pewter smiths), where speciality crafts were on display. Everywhere there were parent-less children who seemed to have escaped from a country where none of its citizens exceeded three feet in height, running and darting in and out of all of the makeshift establishments.

"'Watch out for cut-purses,' said a voice in Dormoy's left ear, as Gaudin made to grab him from behind, before he was aware that the two of us from rue St Victor had reached the rendezvous point. My left arm was in a makeshift sling, my wrist having suffered a sprain in the gallantry of the previous evening. Gaudin had no visible wounds, but his usually confident stride was broken by a decided limp, the result of what he would only describe as a groin injury. 'You're an easy mark,' Gaudin continued, not letting his evident pain stifle his spirits. 'Thieves look for country bumpkins like you who spend their time gawking about them and not looking after themselves.'

"'Oh leave him alone,' I pleaded, having realized that I was doing a little gawking myself at that precise moment.

"'Must you trouble the boy about everything?' It was the heavily accented voice of Testagrossa, who, fresh from morning mass, had just joined the group and saw that the order of the day was to gang up on Gaudin. The young Italian was quite a sight, his skull swathed in a bandage that looked more like a Turkish turban, making his head look even larger than usual. Like four war veterans looking for their severance pay, we stood for a moment admiring each other's injuries and complimenting each other on how bad we looked! Then it was time to see what the great city had to offer.

"Food, of course, was everywhere and reasonably priced for student budgets, so today was sure to be satisfying to our stomachs. There were crepes from Lille, sausages from Lorraine and plentiful ale from Bruges to wash it all down. I didn't do badly for a man with only one hand with which to manage my victuals, but there were also other distractions for all senses and appetites.

"As we turned into one side street, we saw a small, raised clearing on which was situated a kind of spit, a crude affair composed of two forked stakes between which a cross bar was suspended. Tied and bound to the cross piece was a large grey cat, looking as terrified as a witch at Sheffield. A brazier, underneath the spit, was alight with a wood fire that had burned down to white hot coals. At a signal to the audience for silence, two ruffians lifted either end of the cross piece out of the fork and slowly lowered it closer and closer to the brazier. As they did so, the poor captive creature let out a plaintive screech, first of fear then of genuine pain. I turned away in revulsion, all the time cupping my hands over my ears to block out the hellish howl. As I turned, I caught sight of Dormoy, at the far end of the street where an alley, closed and dark even in the daytime, bent to the left and downward toward still more secret places. Dormoy was on his knees, white as a sheet, puking what was left of his Alsatian sausage into the downward sloping gutter. Gaudin and Testagrossa were on either side of him, holding his arms lest he fall forward into his own vomit. By common consent, we headed as rapidly as we could back to the main boulevard, just as soon as Dormoy had some colour restored to his face and was able to stand and walk again.

"Once on the St Germain and after putting sufficient distance between ourselves and the sadistic ritual we had just witnessed, we at last came to rest before a stand that was selling jars of golden honey as well as plum, raspberry and blackberry preserves. A young girl was dipping a stick into an open jar of honey and offering it to us as a sweet, sinless enticement, when another group walked up slowly behind us. I immediately recognised the Huguenot family from the previous evening, the youngest of which was neatly bandaged on the tip and bridge of her nose. She was holding her mother's hand, but upon seeing the four of us, she slid her hand free and walked straight up to the broad shouldered Italian with the big white turban on his head. She reached up, to encircle one of his tree trunk legs in gentle embrace. Then she raised her eyes, intensely searching his sad face with her own clear and jubilant eyes, and said: '*Dieu vous benisse!*' ('God bless you!').

"Testagrossa smiled at her, the way a father looks at his daughter on her wedding day. 'What is your name?' he asked her.

"'*Je m'appelle Clotilde*,' ('I call myself Clotilde,') she said.

"Testagrossa took his large right hand and gently placed it over the child's clean white bonnet. 'God bless you too, Clotilde,' he said, while tracing the sign of the cross over her head.

"The mother, having purchased a jar of honey, turned and offered it to Testagrossa. 'Signor Giambelli, this in no way repays our debt to you all.'

"The young Italian opened the jar and took one of the sticks that the sales girl was holding out to them. He went down on one knee, dipped the stick into the jar and offered it to Clothilde. 'You take good care of your family now, you hear me?' he said ever so gently, as the little girl nodded and took the stick in her small hand. Quickly she put the honeyed end of the stick into her mouth.

"We watched as the family walked on, the little Clotilde holding the honey stick in her mouth long after the last traces of sweetness had gone. Gaudin, Dormoy and I couldn't resist dipping our fingers into the honey, as well. I stopped, nonetheless, long enough to watch the little family disappear into the milling crowds. 'I wonder,' I said to no one in particular, 'what that family would have done if we had not had the good fortune to be there?'

"Before anyone could respond, however, someone pushed past us in his determination to reach the street leading out from the other end of the St Germain. The stranger made contact with Gaudin's shoulder, who pivoted to balance himself, thus colliding with Testagrossa, who reached out to my good arm, making me lose balance and, unable to right myself, fall backward only to be caught by Dormoy.

"When it was over, none of us was quite sure whom we had all seen! He was gone, in the blink of an eye, and despite the series of mishaps he had caused, he had managed to escape without anyone's having had a good look at him.

"Once upright on my own feet, I stood perfectly still. For a moment, I thought I had seen—I could have sworn that I had seen my father, but that was, of course, ridiculous.

"Testagrossa realized that my face had suddenly turned deathly pale. 'Are you all right? You look as if you've just seen a ghost!'

"'I'm fine,' I said, without conviction. I no longer felt terrified. I can only imagine that a distracted, distant look had taken the place of fear on my face.

"'Who was that stranger, and what was his hurry?' asked Dormoy.

"'He looked like the Devil to me,' commented Testagrossa, remarking about his long black cloak, his pointed red-and-grey beard and his stooped shouldered gate.

"'He was a doctor, a learned man,' suggested Gaudin, 'judging from what looked, to me, like academic robes to go with his physician's cap.'

"'His hands!' I raised my finger, as if I had just noticed an important detail. 'Did you see those long, thin fingers stretched out in front of him as if he was afraid of bumping into something?'

"'Where was he going that he needed to forge a path through us to get there?' asked Dormoy for the second time.

"Gaudin was pointing to the intersecting street on the opposite side of the boulevard. 'Whatever it is, it's down that way.' Curiosity having gotten the better of all of us, we headed together towards the narrow street down which the mysterious robbed figure had vanished a few moments earlier.

"The street was crowded with a slightly better dressed mix of revellers than had been in evidence on the main boulevard. They were not milling aimlessly around, either. Rather, they were moving in an orderly fashion in the direction of another descending street, at the entrance to which another large crowd had already assembled. The four of us moved down to take places among the gathering crowd, where we saw a sign, previously covered up by onlookers, on which was posted an announcement about a play to be enacted in the adjoining street, the performance to begin in several moments. The acting troop identified itself as '*Les Confrères de la Passion*', and the piece to be performed, in 3 acts, was called '*La Reine de Poison, ou le Meurtre de Gonzago*' ('The Queen of Poison, or The Murder of Gonzago'), by an anonymous poet, after the tradition of Etienne Jodelle.

"'Oh, I know the argument of this play,' said Dormoy, who evidently enjoyed theatre, among the other wonders of this magnificent city. 'It is about this great lady who dresses remarkably like our Italian Queen, in high heeled shoes like the *putains* of St. Séverin. She has a daughter of marriageable age who is trying to decide between two suitors, one of whom is the son of a very wealthy merchant and financier, while the other is a nobleman of exalted title but, regrettably penniless.'

"'While pondering her alternatives, the great lady visits an old crone who sells love potions and charms, when she's not reading tarot cards or dissecting chickens. The old woman proposes a simple solution to her problem. Let her daughter marry the wealthy merchant, whose fortune she will inherit upon her husband's demise, thereupon she can marry the titled nobleman and have the best of both!'

"'Of course, the success of this scheme depends on being able to assure the timely death of the first husband. That is where the old crone's wares come into play. She offers the great lady a small bottle of very effective poison which she has merely to slip into the evening drink of the first husband before he retires. By morning, the bereaved widow is both wealthy and free to marry her nobleman.'

"At this, all eyebrows arched knowingly, and our four heads drew closer in a single motion.

"This was enough encouragement for Dormoy. 'Of course, the daughter is totally innocent of all of these machinations. The mother must do this on her own, all the while shedding tears for the fragile life of her first son-in-law. She's a magnificent, duplicitous villainess who is both booed and admired by her riotous audience.'

"'Sounds like a play worth seeing,' said Gaudin to the nodding ascent of the whole company.

"Thus intent on loving and hating this creature of the stage, we moved down the street, until we saw, at a dead end, a raised platform, the length of two town houses, upon which were arranged a set of structures intended to represent dwellings in different parts of the city.

"The sets were more suggestive than representative of these things, but they seemed to develop form as different performers, in costume, moved from one side to the other, insuring that props were placed exactly where they needed to be. In back of the platform, mostly concealed by the sets, were two trumpeters and a drummer, ready to signal the start of action with the proper flourish. As the four of us established standing room for ourselves as close to the platform as we could get, the trumpets sounded for silence, and the Prologue came to centre stage to speak his opening lines.

"The costumes, the speeches, the gestures moved in a world of their own and in the imagined world within my mind. I saw the Great, Stately Lady moving with such grace and purpose among a collection of small men with large noses, circling about her. As scene shifted to scene, I was enthralled by the spectacle of sight and sound, but mostly by the sweep and majesty of language that flowed and ebbed from the actors' mouths across to where I stood, transfixed by the magic of it all. When the Great Lady stepped forward to deliver her soliloquy of murderous resolve, I felt the power of her exaltation and of her utterly sublime villainy. I resolved, at that very moment, that I would become a poet of the stage, to bring the resonant sounds and sights of the English theatre to hitherto untested heights.

"And to put this resolve to immediate proof, I have added, to today's entry of my journal, an English rendering of the "Queen of Poison" soliloquy as I both remember from the French and have freely adapted it to have it proclaimed on the English stage:

'So, shall I strike, e'er yet another day
Hath torn to shreds the misty cloak of night
That shrouds the darkest deeds of men and beasts.
Now let nocturnal camp fires' rising fumes
Blot out the light of stars upon my steps
That e'en the powers of Hell's dark Lord, himself
May neither hint nor trace of me belie!
For now must I convince my child to wed
First time, the man of wealth who nightly drinks
A draft of wine, e'er coming to his bed.
Thus on that most auspicious of all nights,
Must I into the wedding chamber steal.
And in the master's cup one drop conceal
The dross of death, the distillation of eternal sleep.
Come Hecate, thou Queen of darkest depths,
Anoint my head, my breast, my purpose cold,
With icy fingers grip my woman's heart,
That hardened, my resolve and strength may stay.
So with a hand as steadfast as my love

Will I from wedding widowhood convey,
And thus with wealth along with tears impart
And clear the path to second marriage bed,
Where title, state and station all converge
With 'heritance of fortune's finest gold.
So may a husband nevermore awake
'Til I his fortune from his bosom take.'

"The "Queen's" sublime theatrical moment was destined to end, however, much as the previous night had ended for the four of us. For out of the hushed silence that befell the unruly crowd of groundlings in the wake of the afore-mentioned speech, a company of equestrian guards cut a path down the descending street to the platform and loudly announced their intention to arrest and detain the entire company of the *Les Confrères de la Passion* until the guild had paid a sizeable fine for having defamed the person of Her Majesty, Catherine Queen of the French.

"Despite my particular enthusiasm for the players' work, we saw, with a certain pragmatism, the futility of trying to duplicate the previous night's acts of heroism, deciding instead to depart from that place, quickly and quietly. We joined the tide of spectators who jostled and shoved one another in their haste to put as much distance as possible in the least amount of time between themselves and the *Duc*'s guard.

While deftly turning left, then right, to avoid leading shoulders and flailing arms amid a sea of murmurs and oaths, I was arrested by the touch of long cold fingers and the cry of a voice as bitter and melodramatic as those of the stage had been. I turned to see the four cornered cap, the searing black eyes, the long face and the pointed grey beard of the strange man we had followed to this place. 'Defend her, you churls, defend the Italian bitch, the Florentine strumpet who plots to put her whimpering little cubs on the throne of France!' He had a look of exaltation on his time ravaged face, and I was sure that, while staring fixedly right at me, the stranger did not, for a moment, actually see me. 'The King of Navarre alone will prevail' he said into the fleeing crowd within which no one seemed to listen and hear, except me. 'The King of Navarre alone will prevail. The King of Navarre will prevail.'

"Dormoy matched my gaze, following the robbed figure as he hobbled away into the milling crowd. 'What did he say, that crazy old man?'

"I couldn't take my eyes away from the fleeing figure, and I couldn't forget those piercing black eyes. 'Something about an Italian bitch and a king in Navarre or Aragon or some such place.'

"'He seemed really angry that the play was interrupted by the *Duc de Guise*'s men,' observed Testagrossa, who was still looking back toward the elevated platform. He noted that the soldiers were amusing themselves by clubbing the actors who lay prostrate at their feet, their hands and arms raise helplessly above their heads.

"'That's the same mad man who nearly knocked us all over to get down there!' said Gaudin, who had pushed ahead and had circled back to see what was holding everybody up.

"I was beginning to understand what I had just witnessed. 'I think it was the story – the Queen – that fascinated him. He was cheated out of the chance to see her get what was coming to her.'

"The sea of souls was beginning to thin and slow down to the normal bustle. Having had enough of the stink and contact of the crowds, we decided to head down to the quay to watch the quiet flow of the Seine and feel the welcome breeze coming off of the river."

***

Thus Howard recorded, in significant detail, the two days during which these events took place. I leafed through several more pages, after these entries, to see if Howard said anything about having gone back to *St. Severin* to resume his encounter with the dark haired, blue eyed prostitute. I found no reference in any subsequent entry that would either confirm or deny that such a second essay had even taken place. I did, however, find a single folded sheet of paper, pressed between two blank pages not far from the entries to which I have just referred. What I found on that sheet, in Howard's careful and steady hand, was the following sonnet, written simply "To Julie...One Evening":

'Thou comest on the shadowed wings of night,
Thy tresses black as mid-night raven's cloak.
Thy crimson robe, thy milky flesh, delight,
Thy fragrance, sweet as rising incense smoke.
Yet from thine eyes the light of mid-day burns,
Two orbs as crystal blue as summer's sky.
For these twin brilliant pools my soul still yearns,
My body trembling, as if wont to die.
Thy lips, like fragrant flowers open wide
To whisper wordless oaths of passion's fire,
And bids me drink, while close to thee I bide,
Thirsting so to quench my chief desire.
In lightest dark, in coldest heat, we live,
'Til we, to one another's passions give."

"As I read these lines over and over again, my mind returned to the scene of trembling at the steps of *St Severin*, and I was satisfied that I had, in fact, read the next chapter of that story."

Chapter 9
An Important Verification

Hank had left a message proposing that we meet at the Guinness pub for dinner. She ended the voicemail with two words: "They match," then she hung up.

So, she, herself, was so excited that she couldn't wait until dinner time to tell me. The expert handwriting analysis had confirmed that the journal was genuine – that it was written in the hand of Henry Howard, the son of the Earl of Surrey. More than that, her forensic specialist's investigation of the paper sample had indicated that it was made, in large part, from hemp, which was a common practice in the 16 century and resulted in paper of a more cloth-like consistency than that which was later considered suitable for printing presses and book binding machines. Likewise, the rust marks that remained of the faded ink were indicative of an iron sulphate and gall formula that was in use in Europe since the 12th century but had rarely been used since the early 1600s, because of the corrosive effect of the iron oxides on wood pulp based paper.

I was restless, and I needed to get out of my hotel room to take some air. I had gone to a book store on the rue de la Quai the day before, where I bought a lithograph copy of a map of Paris from the 1560s. I was looking at some of the place names to which Howard referred in his journal, and I recognized some of the still-standing landmarks, mostly churches.

The first place I visited was the Church of *Saint-Séverin*, where today there are only groups of students sitting on the steps. I walked the narrow winding streets, leading from there in every direction, where nowadays you pass one after another of the store front Greek gyro places, each displaying shards of lamb on giant vertical roasting spits. On street corners, people congregated to listen to string ensembles of conservatory students playing Vivaldi's "Spring".

I knew that neither rue St. Victor nor the *Collège du Cardinal Lemoine* still existed, but the traces and memories of what had been there remain. Where St. Victor had once been, the rue du Cardinal Lemoine descends the hill from the rue des Ecoles to the river, two blocks from the Quai de Notre Dame. In place of the *Collège du Cardinal Lemoine*, there stands today a large post office, a string of boutiques, a coiffure's shop and a courtyard surrounded by apartments. The south wall of these apartments forms the side of a theatre, originally constructed under Napoleon, burned down during the Franco-Prussian War and rebuilt by Gustav Eiffel during the building boom occasioned by the Exhibit of 1898. The theatre's flashing marquee proudly proclaims that this is *"Le Paradis Latin,"* a dinner club in the 19th Century tradition of French cabaret, in a quarter where intellectual pursuits join hands with man's capacity to imagine and to take pleasure in life.

I thought I would propose to Hank that we go there to celebrate our findings and give her the first of the pages I had written - the story I was putting together, based on the diary – just to see what she thought. I walked to rue Monge and turned down a descending side street, past a small Greek restaurant to a tiny triangle of a park; where I sat on a bench and reread the section I had finished that morning.

Chapter 10
A Glimpse at the Finer Life

Journal Entry

"**B**y now, the four of us had become inseparable. We frequently met on the quay, just below where rue St Victor emptied into the street that skirted the river's edge. As we faced the water, to our left stood the graceful length of Notre Dame, her twin steeples pointing steadfastly toward the heavens, like two long fingers of an outstretched hand. The Lady stood on her very own island, the site of the first human settlement, here, separated by water and mist from the bustle of the sprawling city.

"Testagrossa told me that when Julius Caesar first came here in 56BC, he found, on that very spot, a shrine to which Gallic pilgrims journeyed from distant villages to ask their druids to offer sacrifice and seek the favour of the gods and goddesses. Caesar tore down the shrine and built a temple to Juno on top of its ruins, so that his own men could worship the guardian of mother Rome. For Testagrossa, this was always, and always would be, a holy place, dedicated to a holy mother.

"Directly in front of us was a stone bridge joining the left bank of the Seine, on which we were standing, with another island, a smaller one just behind the island where the Cathedral stood. It was a quiet little place called *"Isle Aux Vaches"*. I liked to think of the island as a pastoral setting in the midst of a city, a place of green grass and groves of elms and walnut trees, instead of cobble stones.

"On this particular day, the island was seething with activity, as its grassy fields and shady groves played host to none other than King Henry II, himself, and, it seemed, the entire court. On a beautiful spring morning the King had decided to spend the day on the river, only to be followed by a small fleet of covered barges, overflowing with courtiers and sycophants in their best finery out to see and be seen.

They had come up river from the Louvre and had decided to moor the barges along the shoreline of *Isle aux Vaches*. There, an army of servants who accompanied them set about putting down blankets and laying out bounteous supplies of food and drink. Brightly dressed lute players and flautists, who had supplied music during the cruise up river, disembarked and began to play for the gathering open-air feast.

The royal barge slowed and circled the island, waiting for the preparations to be completed. We guessed that it was the King's barge because it was half again as large as the others with ten oarsmen on each side and a blue canopy trimmed with golden *fleurs de lys* and emblazoned with the Valois family crest. At the stern, and facing the two rows of oarsmen, sat a burley looking man in bright livery with a drum between his thighs. As he beat the drum slowly, one stick in each hand, the oarsmen dipped their oars in unison and cut a path through the water. A lute player sat about mid-ship facing and playing for the person or persons concealed under the canopy. Another, smaller barge followed behind, apparently waiting to land only after the King. This smaller barge also had a royal blue canopy and the Valois family crest, but there was another, smaller crest beneath it, on which were prominently displayed three golden spheres.

"'That must be the Queen and her children,' said Dormoy, as the four of us continued to watch the spectacle.

"Finally, the royal barge made a turn and headed for a narrow landing on the island. Immediately, pages in blue livery emerged from among the revellers and began unrolling a rich red carpet, trimmed in blue and gold, creating a walkway from the beach to a spot of high ground upon which a pavilion had just been erected. Three companies of soldiers simultaneously went into motion: the first lining up on either side of the carpet, the second forming a half moon around the pavilion and the third securing both sides of the stone bridge from the left bank, not far from where we stood gaping at them.

"All eyes were fixed on the barge as it came to ground, the pilot throwing a line to a waiting servant who secured the line to a post as another servant lowered the gang plank into place. Trumpeters, from among the honour guard, set off a flourish as the King emerged, dressed tastefully in cloth of gold, trimmed in blue and ermine, a ponderous gold chain around his neck and a fashionable feathered cap on his head.

"He was tall and well built, for someone just past the prime of his manhood, and he turned to make a courtly gesture to the woman who appeared behind him, offering her a white gloved and bejewelled hand. The woman, herself tall and stately, looked overcome by the gentle solicitude of one so much greater than herself. She had thick black hair, peeking out from the pearl lined hood of her cloak, richly embroidered in cloth of gold. She diminutively bowed her head and accepted the King's outstretched hand.

"'That's Lady Diane *de Poitier*, the King's mistress,' Dormoy whispered conspiratorially into my ear. 'In public, the Queen pretends not to notice her husband's affection for Lady Diane. If that's the case, she's the only one in France – in the world – who doesn't notice it.' With a wave of his hand, Dormoy concluded his commentary on the state of royal matrimony and fidelity.

"I noted that the King's face, in profile, emphasised the prominence of his large, Valois nose. As the couple processed along the carpeted path to the pavilion, people cheered and bowed, and musicians filled the air with sounds of joyous revelry. All this time, the smaller barge waited until the King and his lady were safely in their tent before venturing toward shore for a quiet and respectful but almost unnoticed landing.

"Gaudin regarded our open mouthed fascination with the sneering appraisal of a man of the world. 'So this is how the great and powerful live? You belong to the privileged class, *Monsieur* Worthy Howard,' he continued, feeling the need to needle someone. 'Does the English nobility party and promenade like this on your river, Thames?'

"'My father kept us in the country, while he tended his lands,' I answered, feeling somewhat regretful about it all. 'He never took us to court and I never met women who dress and move like that,' I added, with emphasis.

"'God gives you one face and you paint yourselves another,' said Testagrossa, in undisguised disapproval.

"Dormoy appraised the spectacle with a certain brooding detachment. 'Still, the faces are pleasing, even beguiling.'

"Gaudin raised his index finger and began shaking it close to my face. 'These are the women to whom you should write your poetry, Howard - if you think you are destined to move in such circles - instead of pining in verse over Julie *La Putain*!'

"Testagrossa winced at the epithet. He furrowed his brow but said nothing.

"I only reflected on my lack of prospects, owing to the fact that I am a man of noble birth without title, without land and, at present, without a country.

"Dormoy wore a distant expression on his face. 'Look at the river,' he mused out loud. 'It flows the same for the poor as it does for the wealthy! To me, the waters are like Destiny itself, into which a lady of station may plunge to her death as easily as a common woman.' I wondered if Dormoy might have been thinking of a particular common woman.

"'For my part, I prefer a more accessible class of woman,' said Gaudin, pensively. 'You know that Nature ordains three orders of the gentle sex: ladies of station – alluring and mysterious but inordinately protected by fathers, chaperones and nunneries and, in any event, inaccessible to one of my station; common whores, such as the sisters of *Saint-Séverin*, among whom there is always a selection for every budget; and, in between, the daughters of burghers, shop keepers and inn keepers, respectable enough, but not too respectable to be unavailable. Take, for example, our dear Caterina of the *Ecurie*...'

"'That will be quite enough on that score,' interjected Testagrossa, trying, as always, to raise the level of conversation. 'I'll have you know that Caterina Botelli, for one, was not born to wait on tables. Giovanni Botelli, her father, was a painter and sculptor from Lucca. He was brought to France by the old King François with a commission to paint the great banquet hall at Fontainebleau. He brought his wife and daughter with him, and they lived well under the King's patronage in a comfortable country cottage near the palace. Signor Botelli was a liberal minded man, and he insisted on providing a classical education for his beloved daughter. She learned Latin and Greek, as well as stitching and weaving, so that she could one day take her place among the country gentry and marry into that class.'

"Gaudin was beside himself with amusement at the thought that our Father Testagrossa was in possession of such precise family history concerning Caterina. 'There's more than meets the eye about you, my large headed friend.'

"Testagrossa ignored him. 'The King was evidently pleased with Botelli's work and, on one occasion, gave the artist a golden broach upon which was embossed his own emblem, a fire breathing salamander, on a field of golden fire that did not consume him. Botelli gave the broach to Caterina, reminding her that to aspire to beauty and greatness was not without its dangers. For Caterina, it is her treasure, her most prized possession.'

"I gave Testagrossa a knowing look. 'He gave her a keepsake, a token of his love for her.'

"The Italian nodded his agreement. 'Then, three and a half years into his commission, Signor Botelli fell from his scaffolding at Fontainebleau and broke his neck. King François felt sorry for his wife and daughter and continued to pay the widow a pension as long as he lived. But when King Henry ascended to the throne, on his father's death, he cut off the widow's pension, and the family was left to fend for itself.'

"Dormoy joined in with his brooding, melancholic, hang-dog face. 'So they fell from a life at court to waiting on tables?'

"'They could no longer afford the country cottage, so they moved to Paris, where the mother took in wash and the daughter, to whom the Blanchards took a liking, began in the kitchens for *L'Ecurie*. Between the two of them, the family could maintain a respectable, if poorer style of life, but this is not the life to which they were born, for which they were destined.'

"'Destiny can, indeed, be cruel and capricious,' said Dormoy.

"'If there is such a thing as Destiny,' added Gaudin. "

***

They stayed, throwing stones in the water, to see how far the ripples would spread, until the royal pageant started loading back onto its barges for the return trip down river to the Louvre. By this time, the four friends were, once again, hungry, so, while Testagrossa went to hear Vespers, the others opted for a nearby tavern, by the name of "Cutters," for some supper. Howard noted in his journal entry, at this point, that he could no longer remember why they had chosen this particular tavern that late afternoon, but he remarked that the choice was fortuitous, in that it provided the occasion for their third encounter with the strange, dark robed doctor with the scholar's cap and the pointed red and grey beard.

The story of that encounter was, in fact, the journal entry to which I had randomly opened when I had first laid hands on the leather covered book. I re-read the lines in which Howard described the old man's having fixed them with his penetrating stare, as if he were drawing them into his sphere with those piercing black eyes. He describes their having been irresistibly, almost hypnotically drawn to the empty stools at his table, where he proceeded to introduce himself as Doctor *Michel de Nostra Dame* (or *Notre Dame*, in modern French), the very same Michaelus Nostradamus whose book of quatrains had been circulating among the salons of the privileged and the hovels of students since its publication three years before.

The University had forbidden all lectures and public discussions of the book, which, of course, meant that every student made the effort to procure the book and read it. Despite his notoriety, however, Doctor Michel made it very clear to his new acquaintances that they were to tell no one of their encounter with him, nor even disclose that they had any knowledge of him or of his presence in Paris.

The Queen, he told them without their having asked, had heard of his reputation in Provence and had commanded that he come to court, earlier in the year, to consult with her concerning the horoscopes of her children. Others at court, however, including the King and his all-powerful cousins, the *Duc de Guise* and *Guise'* brother, the Cardinal of Lorraine, did not share her majesty's admiration for astrologers and other practitioners of the occult. Doctor Michel was warned that if he were to show his face in the capital again, a warrant would be sworn out for his arrest, and the Queen was unwilling to offend her husband and his powerful cousins by granting him the same protection she had offered to the Italian astrologers in her entourage.

"So I left the city, and when she sent word that she required my presence for yet another consultation, I was convinced that she was preparing to feed me to the pack of scavengers who, like skulking, salivating dogs, follow the Valois lion. I hid from her messengers, hid in the one place they would not look for me, right under their large and bulbous noses, here in Paris."

So he rambled on, repaying Howard's reluctant stare with a vision of his father's untimely execution. He continued, addressing nobody in particular, oblivious to the very presence of Howard and his friends, when all of a sudden, he fixed his gaze upon Dormoy, whose grey, melancholic eyes met the black, piercing stare of the suddenly silent old man. It was as if all other thought and concern had suddenly vanished from his wandering consciousness.

Silence enveloped them all as the old man raised a bony finger and spoke directly to Dormoy, as if the boy's very soul were draped out there in the candle light in front of him. He spoke with a thick local accent, as if he were dredging up the details of his own past, when everyone spoke like that. He spoke in calm and measured tones, reciting, as it were, from a text or some rehearsed lines. All the same, his voice was choked with the immediacy of what he saw with his interior eye. "The plague," he croaked, "wearing a black hooded cloak and carrying a crooked stick, took your mother, in the prime of her youth and would not listen to your cries for mercy. He will take another whom you continue to love. You can neither save her nor stop loving her."

Dormoy crumbled on his stool and lowered his face into his hands while, from deep in his chest, a long suppressed cry issued forth through his muffled lips, like the plaintive bleating of a rabbit being slaughtered. Howard wrote no more of that night's encounter, but I cannot imagine that any of them, not even Gaudin, could have broken the dark silence with any further conversation.

Almost every entry in Howard's journal, thereafter, made some mention of Doctor *Michel de Nostra Dame*. He haunted Howard's imagination, like some terrifying spectre that he dared not confront alone and unprotected by his group of friends.

Dan Scannell

Chapter 11
The Discovery of a New World

Journal Entry

"Dormoy, I had begun to observe, had been quick to hold his terror in check and had become morbidly curious about the kinds of forbidden things that this man must know. Was this the 'New Learning' that has come bursting forth from the rediscovery of what the Greeks and Arabs knew a thousand years ago? Did Doctor Michel possess medicinal and arcane secrets and procedures that could cure the plague, as people were saying about him? Did he have visions of the future as clear as his knowledge of the past?

"Testagrossa didn't think so. 'You don't really believe that he sees the future, do you?' he asked rhetorically, with his best theological frown, 'that there are things which are destined to happen, no matter what we do to forestall them? What, then, is free will, if our life's courses are determined by an inexorable fate, no matter what we do? That would mean that none of us is responsible, either for his actions or for their consequences!'

"Gaudin looked amused, as usual, searching for the practical side of every question. 'That would be convenient. If anything goes wrong, we can always blame it on Fate and say it was out of our hands.'

"'Still, we would want to take the credit if something were to turn out well, wouldn't we?' I added, trying to take the conversation to the next level. 'We can't very well take authorship of our successes if we blame Destiny for our failures, can we?'

"'I suppose not,' said Dormoy, 'but, if there is no fixed or predetermined future, then what is it that he sees, assuming he sees anything at all?'

"I seized upon the question. 'If we see the past, as if looking in a mirror, at what is already behind us, we can say that we are viewing something that truly was, and if we see it accurately, it should always look the same, regardless of what we do as a consequence. If we view the future, however, as in a window in front of us, through which we see that which has not yet arrived, what is it that we see, if it never happens because we subsequently alter what otherwise would have been our chosen course of action?'

"'It's not the future,' admitted Dormoy, 'because it is not what will eventually happen.'

"'It's nothing' said Gaudin, 'but shadows and dreams.'

"'Then, are they real, or just our imagination?' I asked.

"That was when I noticed a marked change in the hitherto withdrawn and passive behaviour of my Provençal friend. Dormoy began voraciously seeking out anything that smacked of the occult or any area of knowledge that was forbidden, discouraged or in any way discredited by conventional academia.

"As if awakened from a kind of melancholic stupor, Dormoy began suggesting visits and outings. He began pestering Testagrossa to arrange a meeting with Brother Anselm, the pharmacologist at the Abbey of *Sainte-Geneviève*, where he harangued the helpful monk with a barrage of questions about the medicinal uses of this or that herb and all of the derivatives and poultices that he knew to be effective in treating fevers and skin eruptions.

"Anselm told him it was all to be found in ancient volumes, translated from the Arabic back in the 12th century and carefully preserved in the enormous library of *Sainte-Geneviève*. After much pestering, the master of herbal remedies agreed to introduce him to Brother Lawrence, the librarian. With both Testagrossa and Anselm as character references, Dormoy was able to gain entry for the four of us to the abbey's massive library.

"Between the Chapter House and the abbatial church, rose a long "T" shaped building looking, from the outside, very much like a church without a steeple. Behind ponderous oak doors, set in a large, bas-relief ornamented central pointed arch and two smaller arches, stretched a long rectangular room with a high, vaulted Gothic ribbed ceiling and bounded by walls supported externally by flying buttresses. The walls were almost entirely taken up with a series of high, pointed windows, with clear, transparent glass panes, the better to bath the room in natural illumination throughout the daylight hours. There was a central aisle, on either side of which stood rows of long, heavy, oak tables and tall, straight backed oak chairs.

"Some of the tables featured portable lecterns, to hold volumes for reading and copying. We could also discern ink wells and quills, together with small thin bladed knives and blotting pads. There were only about three or four monks apparently copying that day, and eight or nine more reading and scribbling notes on small pieces of slate.

"Directly inside the main entrance, the four of us and Brother Anselm were met by a tall, thin monk in his early thirties, with a thick mop of reddish brown hair, surrounding his tonsure, threatening at any moment to overrun it. Anselm had, of course, told him to expect visitors, and he welcomed us with a broad smile and a wave of recognition for the lumbering, dark haired Italian.

"'Welcome to our scriptorium and reading room,' said the affable librarian, drawing his hand in a circle towards the expanse of the room about them. 'Here is where we copy the books we have borrowed, before returning them.' He was gesturing left and right, as they walked down the central aisle, the full length of the large room.

"'The great monastic libraries of Europe (of which we are one of the foremost) used to have an elaborate exchange program going on for centuries. Otherwise, if you wanted to read a particular work that was held in the library at Bologna, for example, you had to go to Bologna to read it, which is, of course, not at all practical. So what we did was to make lists of the books that we had, and the other libraries made lists of what they had. Then we would do an exchange of the books we wanted and copy the books we had borrowed, before returning them to the library from which we had borrowed them. This way, works could be made available all over and not just in one collection.

"'Of course, now that Paris and other major cities have licensed printers and modern presses, books are made available much faster and our little network is no longer needed. Still, we have some famous illuminists whose work remains in demand. Do you see old Brother Norbert, over there? He's been copying a Latin edition of Plutarch's *Lives of the Noble Greeks and Romans* for over three years now. His eyes are starting to go, though, and I guess that Plutarch's *Lives* will be his last book.'

"'I never knew that librarians were allowed to talk so much!' commented Gaudin, with a grin directed at Testagrossa.

"Brother Lawrence let out a hearty laugh. 'Please forgive my going on like this,' he replied, still relishing his own laughter. 'Mine is a mostly silent profession. So when I get a new audience, I take full advantage of it.'

"By then, they had walked the length of the scriptorium's central aisle, at the end of which was an interior, bas-relief covered façade surrounding another ponderous oak door. This inner portal led into the transept or cross section of the building. Brother Lawrence turned a latch and pushed the door open, using his right shoulder to exert additional force. Before entering, however, he turned to his guests and, indicating a sconce hanging on the wall just to the left of the door, signalled to Testagrossa to take its lighted candle, and hold it for us.

"They stepped from a world bathed in sunlight to a place of perpetual obscurity, the darkness only occasionally relieved by small circular halos of faint yellow candle light. Once their eyes had accustomed themselves to the darkness, they saw, around them, a huge rectangular room lined on all sides by shelf after shelf of books, ranging from the floor to the dizzying heights of the ceiling. On both sides of the room, circular stair cases lead to yet another height where, Brother Librarian told them, there was another room of like dimensions, the walls of which were also filled with books, and above that, yet another, likewise filled with the treasure of centuries.

"Never had I seen so many books in one place before. I stood still, closed my eyes and inhaled deeply.

"'Do you smell that, all of you?' asked Brother Lawrence, a broad smile spreading over his rapturous face. 'That's the smell of old books, the perfume of wisdom, the intoxicating vapours of knowledge, coming down to us from the ages.'

"'I think you're in heaven already, Brother', said Testagrossa, seeing what he imagined to be the transformation that the human face would undergo, overcome by some ecstatic vision.

"'You see a librarian's glimpse of heaven, and his nightmare of the flames of hell! My greatest fear and my constant preoccupation is with fire. Can you imagine how quickly flames could destroy these works, irretrievably? How in an instant, all of these treasures would be lost to us and to future generations, who will visit this spot and find – nothing?

"'Night after night, I wake in a sweat after such terrifying dreams, and I am not there to stop them. I see these books consumed in flames, as angry men and women, with lurid torches in their hands and cries of "Revolution" on their lips, burn this entire edifice to the ground.'

"The librarian's look of ecstasy was replaced by the look of a child, frightened to death of the dark and what he could or could not see within it, and I was reminded, once again, of my own night terrors.

"Dormoy drew us back to palpable reality with his insatiable curiosity: 'How many volumes have you here, Brother?'

"'Over 12,000, after my last cataloguing.' Brother Lawrence felt more himself again, thanks to the distraction of an answerable question. 'Come with me,' he said to us all, his face brightening again with the prospect of another opportunity to share his solitary kingdom.

"He lead us to a small indentation in the shelving that revealed an open alcove, in which there was just enough room for a desk, a straight backed chair and a range of shelves in the wall behind. On the desk we could see a stained blotter, an ink well and quills, and four very large, bound volumes. This, we gathered, was Brother Lawrence's office.

"The librarian pushed aside his writing materials, seized the top most volume and excitedly opened it, facing the book outward, toward us. 'Anyone can collect books and stack them in an old building,' he began, his old ebullience having been completely recovered. 'The real challenge of being a librarian is knowing what you have and being able to locate and retrieve it on demand. That's what separates the great libraries from the dusty, old private collections!'

"Dormoy and I took the candle stick from Testagrossa and leaned in closer to see.

"'Look here – and be careful with that candle. This is a catalogue of every book we have, classified in five ways, according to the ancient system of Aristotle himself, and mapped, by this method, to a particular area and shelf location in the library. Our books are categorised by:

1) Who – the author, if known, according to which we assign it the first two letters of the author's name, followed by,
2) What – the subject to which we have assigned a series of numbers, 1000 – 1999, 2000 – 2999, etc., corresponding, respectively, to Philosophy, Theology, Natural Science, the Poetics, Rhetoric, History, Mathematics and Philology. This number is followed by:
3) Where – two letters for the country where the work was composed, followed by,
4) When - a numeric value for the century of composition, and finally,
5) How – for the language of the version we have on our collection (Greek, Latin, Arabic, Hebrew, or one of the modern vulgar languages). Of course, it's possible to have two versions of the same book: one in Latin and the other in the original Greek, for example, in which case there would be a different language code in the catalogue for each version.'

"'Thus, we can assign a unique value to each volume and assign that value to a unique position in our array of shelves.'

"'And by sharing your catalogue with other libraries," I added, "anyone can know where they can find what they are looking for and what they may want to copy for their own collection.'

"'Except that, if it takes three years to copy one book,' calculated Dormoy, 'depending on how many copyists you have at any one time, it would take hundreds of years to copy all of what you have here.'

"'Librarians are forcibly a very patient breed,' reflected Brother Lawrence. 'And God has given us the printing press to get us out of this dilemma, hasn't He?' concluded the librarian, with a tone of ambivalence, in his voice.

"'And just in time,' reflected Gaudin, thinking of how few of the tables in the scriptorium were actually in use by copyists.

"'Now, let's put this catalogue to the test and see if we can find just what you young scholars are interested in reading today.'

"'I would like to see a copy of Aristotle's *Poetics*.' I was the first to speak up, remembering my resolution upon seeing *The Murder of Gonzago* enacted at the *St Germain* Fair.

"'In Latin or the original Greek?' asked the librarian, happy to have a chance to give an actual demonstration of his catalogue's capacity to enable quick retrievals.

"My Latin is much more serviceable than my Greek, I'm afraid," I admitted.

"'And you?' Brother Lawrence asked of Gaudin, the visibly least impressed of his listeners.

"'I would like a copy of Caesar's *Commentarii de bellum Gallicum*,' he replied, feeling quite impressed with himself."

"'The Latin is simple and sufficiently bloody,' replied the librarian, without much fanfare.

"'I'll take another look at Aquinas' *Summa Contra Gentiles*, said Testagrossa before quickly adding: 'and a copy of the *Carmina* of Catullus.'

"'And what is our young theologian's interest in licentious Roman love poetry?' asked Brother Lawrence, with a raised eyebrow over his still broad smile.

"'I just want to be able to give some advice to young Howard, here, who has taken a hand at writing love poetry of his own,' said Testagrossa, trying to look as disinterested as he could.

"'We always seek to encourage young poets,' mused the librarian with an indulgent smile, 'and young lovers need no encouragement at all.' He lingered a moment with this thought, and then he seemed to dismiss the idea and quickly turned back to his catalogue.

"Dormoy had been silent and pensive, all this time. When Brother Lawrence turned to him, the sad youth's eyes refused to make contact with those of the librarian. 'I'd like to see a copy, in Latin, of the works of *Jabir Ibn Hayyan*. Do you have such a book?'

"'Ah yes, the alchemist, *Geberus*, as we call him in Latin. We have a collection of his works, although they are not included in any course of study of which I am aware. Officially, we do not have these books available for students, but because you are a friend of Brother Anselm and young Giambelli, here, I can make certain titles available for your study. I, myself, have never been of the opinion that books, in and of themselves, are either good or bad, in the moral sense of the term. It depends on what you do with the knowledge that you gain from them.'

"'And what do you plan to do with the knowledge of Alchemy, Claude Dormoy?' demanded Testagrossa, as if the salvation of his immortal soul depended upon his answer.

"'I just want to know.' Dormoy's expression changed from defensive to defiant. 'I want to know more because we understand so little of this vast world, for all our knowledge and learning, and people die every day because we simply do not know how to save them.'

"'There are other ways of saving them and other avenues of knowledge, apart from Alchemy,' suggested Testagrossa.

"'Then I want to know them all, including what is forbidden. I want nothing hidden from me,' said Dormoy, with a decisive setting of his jaw.

"Brother Lawrence shrugged and began searching in his index for the location of the requested volumes. Having made some quick notes to himself, he turned, without a word, and disappeared up the staircase to the left, to the locations he had mapped. We went out again to the scriptorium and found a table where we could spread out and catch the afternoon sunlight, the better to read in comfort.

"After ten minutes, or so, the oak door from the inner sanctum creaked open, and Brother Lawrence re-emerged stooping under the weight of a stack of volumes, which he balanced, like a juggler as he sidled to the table where the four of us had found places. He handed out the books as a mother hands sweets to children, pleased to see them happy but careful to guard against excess. At Dormoy's chair, however, he stopped.

"'Our collection of *Geberus* is actually quite meagre, but here is a compendium, in Latin, simply called *The 112 Books*, containing Geber's version of the *Tabula Smaragdina*.'

"'The Emerald Tablet,' translated Dormoy, his hand cradling the tome, while his fingers traced the lettering on the binding.

"'I'd send you to St. Victor's monastery, just over the wall from the Cardinal Lemoine, but I don't believe their collection is any better. I have another idea, though. I'll go back to my office and write you a letter of recommendation to Brother Sixtus, at the Convent of the Celestines, across the river. I am told he has quite a collection on Alchemy and Astrology that the brothers are holding for the Queen. I'll put in my note to Brother Sixtus that you are doing some research for *Sainte-Geneviève*'s library, and he'll give you all the titles you want.'

"'Thank you, Brother,' mumbled the boy, never raising his eyes from the book in his hand.

"After, once again, caressing, the leather binding as one would sooth a spirited stallion by stroking his neck and mane, Dormoy reverently opened and leafed through the volume. He found the page whereon was sketched an illustration of a luminous tablet of polished green stone embossed with 14 lines of text, like the commandments of another god. The new devotee began to scribble them down, but they were just disjointed phrases, here a clause leading directly into another, there a statement having nothing to do either with what went before or what followed. Perhaps it was a code or secret language that could only be understood by an initiate, or perhaps there really is one true element from which everything, in the heavens, on the earth and below the earth is derived. Perhaps there really is a process by which earth can be distilled from fire, precious substances can be separated from the gross, and the Giver of life itself, with the Sun for its father and the Moon for its mother, sends its eternal gift on the wings of the wind to the womb and heavy breasts of Mother Earth!

"At last recovering from his ecstatic reverie, the self-conscious youth glanced to his right, where Testagrossa's large head hung falcon-like over his own tome. Dormoy more than half expected to see a scowl of theological disapprobation piercing the air between them from his friend's furrowed and prominent brow. Instead, he caught an abstracted, wistful look, as of eyes also focused on some distant and unknowable thing. At the same time, if he was not mistaken, he saw the stocky youth's mouth moving and heard a hushed, rhythmic murmur of words, though he could not make out their meaning. Unable to make any sense of what he was witnessing, Dormoy looked over to where I had also raised my eyes from my contemplation of the willing suspension of disbelief to share the spectacle of Testagrossa in ecstasy.

"I leaned sidelong to get a better look at the open volume in front of my absorbed friend. It was not Aquinas. Oh no; it was none other than Catullus, the Roman poet of erotic love, whose work had so moved the bushy haired youth. I read the lines I could see above the outspread hand of Testagrossa, noting them carefully on my sheet containing some Aristotelian aphorisms and recorded them in my journal, with my own English rendering, as follows:

Passer, deliciae meae puellae, Quicum ludere, quem in sinu tenere, Cui primum digitum dare appententi, Et acris solet incitare morsus. Cum desiderio meo nitenti Carum nescio quid lubet iocari, Et solaciolum sui doloris,	Oh sparrow, delight of my girl. Whom she bounces on her lap in play. With index finger pressing near to thee, Just to provoke sharp, playful bites. All the time, my most ardent desire is To offer her some sort of kindly play, To give solace to her sorrow.

"'Strange,' I reflected, 'that although Dormoy's reverence for the arcane gibberish of alchemy came as no surprise, given his recent strange turn of character, nothing could have prepared me for the spectacle of the thick headed seminarian's becoming transfixed by the image of a girl playing with a pet bird.'

"I found my friend's reverie quite contagious. I thought of Julie, who is definitely not to be paired with a sparrow, or a lark, or any bird found in a maiden's garden warmed by the morning sun. No, Julie would prefer a creature of the night. She would play with the nightingale and not the lark! I was transfixed by the pristine innocence of the scene, the allure of such a moment of secret sweetness.

"I immediately tried to shake off my errant thoughts, reproaching myself for my idleness. It's strange how our minds wander, when we're supposed to be working. This mood, I considered, belongs to daydreams and not to serious study.

"That afternoon, over mutton soup and beer, both Dormoy and I confronted our heavy set friend about the whole incident. We made the mistake, however, of bringing the subject up in front of Gaudin, who had been sitting at the far end of our table and had missed the whole exchange.

"The ring leader roared with laughter, when he heard me read back the lines I had jotted down. 'I'd really like to know what's going on in that fat head of yours.' Gaudin gave the Italian youth an appraising look, as if seeing him in a new light. 'It would be a mistake to underestimate you,' observed Gaudin with something approaching admiration.

"'What's to be concerned about?' Testagrossa lifted his palms carelessly in the air over his head. 'I love birds, as did St. Francis from Assisi,' said the Italian youth, without regard to the other personage in the poem.

"'And do you like to amuse young girls with your easy wit?' Gaudin cut close to the quick, trying to get the appropriate reaction from his friend.

"'I am as renowned for my easy wit as are you for your tact and subtlety,' retorted Testagrossa, having summoned up all of his customary detachment.

"Later that evening, the four of us returned to the narrow streets and alleys that flowed like tributaries into the Place Maubert, to a tavern called *La Coullière de Bois*, a place that had been recommended by an acquaintance of Dormoy's. The tables were of the same rough, unfinished wood that you'd find in almost any other tavern on the Left Bank. We seized upon an obscure table which had some crude lettering carved into the side where I was sitting. On closer examination, it proved to be the Latin expression: '*CAVE CANEM*' ('BEWARE OF THE DOG.') I glanced over at the room's central fireplace, where I discerned what looked like a darker piece of gloom, a kind of shapeless shadow which turned out to be an ancient sheep dog that seemed to have lain in state, on that precise spot, for longer than any of the regular patrons could remember.

"Gaudin caught the eye of a serving wench, who was stepping nimbly over the spreading haunches of the slumbering beast. While returning the youth's glance, she missed a step and landed squarely on the dog's outstretched front leg, spilling a good portion of Belgian lager over the animal's eyes and snout. Although the ruffled waitress was curling her lip and mumbling expletives in the dog's general direction, the beast remained still as death, not so much as twitching under the weight of her foot fall and the sprinkle of beer.

"'Surely,' I thought, 'the creature was either dead or in some kind of comatose state, not even deigning to respond to verbal or liquid insult flung his way, without the slightest provocation on his part. Only in such a state would the beast be able to maintained his peaceful dominion over the damp piece of dirt floor which his dishevelled coat continued to cover.'

"'I think this carved message is intended more for the serving wench than for anyone else in here tonight,' I remarked, as the girl, still scowling, approached our table. She wore a look that announced her clear intention to hurl her contempt upon us, if she could not take out her frustration on the dog.

"'Is there not a little kindness, gentlemen, for one upon whom misfortune has fallen?' It fell, of course, to Testagrossa to say something soothing to assuage her embarrassment, but the mood was spoiled by laughter emanating from the nearby tables.

"Dormoy was the only one of the surrounding company who was neither laughing nor making any effort to assuage the girl's embarrassment. He had put on his familiar absorbed, distracted look, as if he were attending to another scene neither humorous nor near at hand. Gaudin, anxious to deflect everyone's attention from the plight of the angry female, grabbed Dormoy's shoulder, to wrench him back to this time and place.

"'Hey Dormoy, tell us what you were reading this afternoon, so we can be sure to avoid it. This place would be a million laughs if we all put on your long cow face!'

"Dormoy looked about disdainfully and jerked his shoulder free from Gaudin's grasp. 'I can't expect you to understand the mystery of the Oneness of all things, can I?' remarked Dormoy, his eyes lifted above the earthly heads around him.

"'The "Oneness of all things"?' jeered Gaudin, doing his best to imitate Dormoy's Provençal accent. 'Your Master of Gibberish teaches, I take it, that all things in the universe are composed of the same fundamental base element? That fire and earth are the same, that water and air are the same, despite all of our experience to the contrary, despite all that Aristotle and the great masters have taught us for centuries?'

"'He does,' replied Dormoy with quiet, grim determination and that setting of his jaw which I had noted so often in him, of late. 'There is a way, he hints, that with careful separation and re-mixing we can isolate what is the essence of anything and change any substance into another' added Dormoy as if reciting a new and more powerful creed.

"'He "hints"?' Testagrossa seized upon the point as if he had caught his friend in a deliberate lie. 'If this is such an important principle, why does he not say it outright, instead of cloaking his teachings in riddles and an endless series of clues and innuendoes?'

"Dormoy ignored the question, disdaining to elucidate something about which Geber, himself, had with such determination remained silent. Instead, he raced to the next level of speculative wonder. 'What if we can transform evil body humours into good ones? What if we can make diseased organs into healthy members? What if we can make something – someone – already dead, alive again?'

"Testagrossa registered genuine shock and concern, not anger, towards his friend. 'Do you have any idea what you are asking for? I know your intentions are good, Claude, that you want this knowledge, this power, to save lives and not to destroy them, but you are seeking the fruit of the tree of good and evil knowledge, you are seeking the power of Faustus, and you are willing to set loose forces that can turn on you and destroy you!'

"'Doctor Michel commands those forces,' said Dormoy his voice emitting a throaty awe.

"'Yes,' I said, 'and he skulks in terror of the King, the Queen and their entire entourage.'

"'It is the Italian Queen who shares his appetite for forbidden knowledge,' said Dormoy, 'who urges him to share his dark secrets with her.'

"'The Queen can protect herself,' said Gaudin, showing genuine concern for his friend, 'but your uncle is not the Pope and you don't have powerful friends and kin to protect you from the fowl winds that will blow.'

"Dormoy set his face and stuck his jaw out to the world. 'I'm willing to take that chance. Someone has to!'

"I said nothing. My thoughts, upon hearing Dormoy's incredible hypothesis, immediately turned to the image of my father, disappearing down the road for the last time, the whirlwinds of snow kicked up by his horse trailing behind him like smoke from a smouldering fire. 'Call him back,' I thought, 'from the dust of death, from the headsman's axe, from the smouldering fires of time.'

"'You all worry too much,' protested Testagrossa, putting his finger on a theoretical point on the table in front of him. 'You're either re-living the past or struggled to know and reshape the future. If you want to be at peace, find some focal point in the present world, where we are today, and rest your gaze on it. We are alive, now. When we are focused on some tiny spot of beauty, what happened yesterday doesn't matter and what will come tomorrow hasn't been born yet. Stop trying so hard and the light will come to you.'

"'Now you sound like a real mystic,' I said. 'Have you found your centre of peace, my friend?'

"Testagrossa was about to say something, but he stopped himself. 'Not yet' he admitted, looking somewhat deflated at being unable to follow his own advice.

"'Me neither,' I admitted, 'but I hope that my father found such a moment.'

"'I believe he did.' Testagrossa was not simply trying to find comforting words for his friend. His face projected a quiet certainty, so peaceful that it could not have been feigned.

"'I wish I had your faith,' I replied, my voice having descended almost to a whisper.

"'Wishes won't make beggars into knights,' said Gaudin with a dismissive wave of the hand. 'The having is all, and the only certainty is what you can grasp in your hands.'

"'You will always be a blunt instrument in a small surgical theatre,' said Dormoy finally out of patience with the older boy."

***

The candle light must have sputtered out on Howard's makeshift table in the cramped room at the *Collège du Cardinal Lemoine* on rue St. Victor, because the narrative of this day ended abruptly on the yellow and jagged edged page before me.

Chapter 12
Account of a Strange Incident

Journal Entry

"It wasn't long before Dormoy had organized a day trip to the Celestine convent, to further his studies in the Arabic origins of Alchemy and other pursuits, both forbidden and fascinating. It was rare for us to venture across the river, to where our accents would be more noticeable and where no one, but priests and court officials, spoke a word of Latin. Consequently, we decided to meet at the *Ecurie* the evening before to make some precautionary plans.

"First of all, we were to leave our academic robes behind, so as to present a less obvious target for gutter thugs and soldiers, but our street clothes were not at all in fashion with the place, or the time. We finally settled on a stratagem to sport long, riding cloaks to conceal our non-Parisian attire, even though spring had come and gone, and the balmy breeze, wafting from the Seine, would most likely overheat us before we had managed to cross the *Pont St Michel*. We all procured black cloaks with hoods, except for Testagrossa's, which was brown, Gaudin remarked, like a Franciscan's.

"For his part, Testagrossa was taking little or no interest in our preparations, whether out of disapproval of Dormoy's academic pursuits or for some other, unstated reason. I turned, at the mention of the cloaks, and noticed that my Italian friend had removed himself to a separate table, closer to the spiral staircase. He was, at that moment, deep in conversation with the waitress, Caterina, who was leaning on the railing, one foot on the first step of the ascent. Testagrossa was speaking in a low voice, so I could not make out what he was saying, but I noticed that his hands were uncharacteristically still and his face, devoid of animation, was cast in an earnest grimace. I thought that this might very well be the expression that my friend would assume, when he was hearing confessions. Caterina, for her part, did not appear to be very happy with what he was saying, looking almost as if her large, solemn friend might be scolding her.

"Fortunately for Caterina, Marie Blanchard appeared at the top of the stairs, a tray in one hand and the other hand crooked at her hip. The young waitress wasted no time, darting obediently back up the stairs to the kitchen. Testagrossa sat still for a moment, staring into darkness, then he rose slowly and slouched back to the table, just as we three friends were rising, promising to meet early the next morning, in front of *Saint-Severin's*.

"My questions about the little scene I had just witnessed would have to wait for a more appropriate moment the next day.

***

"The right bank was like another world, with wider, freshly paved streets, over which people of quality road on well-groomed horses or in fashionable carriages. The taverns were all up-scale, compared with those of the Latin Quarter, and there were many more lawyers, doctors and courtiers (judging from their dress) than there were friars and nuns to be seen ambling in small groups up and down the main thoroughfares.

"The *Duc*'s guards were very much in evidence here, and people's papers were being checked at many of the intersections of larger and more crowded streets. Once, we were stopped on the *Rue de la Curriere*, at which point Dormoy produced his letter from the Brother Librarian of *Sainte-Geneviève's* Abbey. At the sight of an official looking Latin document, the guard nodded and waived them on in the direction of the convent. We were given another suspicious glance, when we reached the intersection with the *Rue Melville du Temple*, but the guards, in the colourful livery of the House of *Guise*, decided, instead, to stop a farmer's cart, in the hope that they could pilfer something valuable that might be concealed under the pile of hay that was covering the rickety conveyance.

"We continued due east until the street dead-ended at the *Rue des Celestines*, which runs north-south along the wall behind which the convent crouched. To gain access, we would have had to have turned right, in order to enter by the main portico which faced south, but there was such a commotion and bustle of people pushing and shoving its way north from where we could hear the beating of drums and the blare of trumpets. So, we decided, on the spur of the moment, to turn left, instead, and join the melee headed toward whatever spectacle lay in that direction.

"'Cut-purse convention, I see,' said Gaudin, looking at the faces of those who were pushing in around them, but since our heavy cloaks were over our belts and the sacks of coins that hung from them, we considered ourselves safe from thievery.

"When we reached the corner, we saw the object of the pilgrimage. The royal lodgings at *L'Hotel des Tournelles* stood out before them, to the east, in front of which stretched a long tilting yard, on an expansive, oval shaped piece of land just outside the apartments. The centre of the yard had been completely levelled, except that there was a wooden barrier, like a seam, down the centre, to separate two equestrian combatants as they would pass each other at high speed.

"Outside of the central, tilled area, there were clusters of colourful pavilions, resplendent with coats of arms, which caught the sunlight like convex mirrors, topped with multi-coloured, striped and checked pennants that competed with each other for the attention of the dazzled onlookers. Since jousting was clearly a spectator sport, the next ring of the oval was taken up with recently erected wooden bleachers at the east end of which was an elevated reviewing stand. Over the front of the reviewing stand was draped a huge tapestry, dominated by the emblem of a shield: three golden *fleurs de lys*: two on top, one below, on a field of azure.

"Above the Valois tapestry were two throne chairs and some smaller chairs for the privileged few who sat by invitation on the dais with the King and Queen. That day, however, the dais was empty, notwithstanding the fact that the bleachers were packed and bustling with boisterous activity, and the pavilions were already spilling out armoured knights. Grooms were hastening forward with destriers and chargers decked out in colourful caparisons.

"There was a fence at the far end of the oval, behind which we four and the other late comers were pushing and jostling for position. A group of Bretons, who had evidently been celebrating for some time, recognised Gaudin and offered us a place in the front spot they had staked out for themselves earlier. One of them noted that there would be no dignitaries today, because these were just preliminary elimination rounds, to allow some of the younger knights to get some tournament experience. There was however, one knight who was striding from pavilion to pavilion, checking on the positioning of everyone's armour and evidently giving pointers on the tightening of the helmet strap and the securing of the spurs.

"'That's Gabriel, *Comte de Montgomery*, the captain of the King's Scottish guards,' said our Breton host, with the casual air of an expert on these matters. 'He's giving some pointers to the novices on how to keep from breaking their necks the first time they meet an opponent,' he added by way of commentary.

"A young knight was deep in consultation with Montgomery, when a groom brought up a skittish charger, draped in yellow and green. A squire had taken the reins to try to calm the animal. He was struggling, unsuccessfully, to slip a piece of protective iron headgear, which Gaudin said was called a *"chanfron,"* onto the horse's snout. Montgomery immediately intervened, quieting the animal by stroking his neck gently with one hand while mounting the headpiece quickly with the other. He then continued to hold the reins firmly while two attendants helped lift the young knight into the saddle. The first timer was so heavily laden with armour that he could never have mounted the charger by himself.

"Gaudin pointed in the direction of the encumbered knight and his mount. 'That horse isn't so big. You should see the massive beast that Montgomery rides in tournaments. He's half again as tall as this one and nasty as a headache after a night of drinking and carousing,' he added for emphasis. 'They control the animals with the spurs they wear high on their leg plates, to dig into the horses' flanks, and with their thighs, they control direction and movement, since their hands are occupied with weapons. Montgomery has thighs like an Italian whore, and rides with equal confidence and vigour!' He nodded at his friends knowingly, his lips twisted into a leering grin.

"The young knight brought his mount to a steady canter and moved him to the end of the tilt yard closest to the spectators' fence, while another knight was assisted to his charger and positioned himself nearest to the pavilions. Montgomery shouted: 'Aim, then lower your head for contact,'

"The Captain offered his final instructions to the first knight, as the two riders aligned themselves to the central barrier, lowered their solid oak lances into position and spurred their mounts toward each other.

"They really didn't build up great speed, because this pass was about accuracy in positioning the blunted end of the lance on the opponent. Nevertheless, the thumping sound of wood against metal was loud enough to startle Dormoy, who had never before witnessed either real or ceremonial combat and who was sure that he had heard the sound of bone crunching. Neither rider was unhorsed, but one had apparently nearly missed the neck of his opponent's horse, which, in addition to being uncomfortable for the animal, would have caused the beast to rear in protest and almost certainly throw and seriously injure the rider.

"'Aim for the shield; I told you to AIM!' shouted Montgomery, his hands gripping the horse's reins to hold him firmly but gently while he upbraided the youth, still sitting high in the saddle. 'Two more passes with lances,' Montgomery said to both combatants, 'and the only bruises I want to see should be born by you! Do I make myself clear?'

"The next two passes showed perfect form, on the part of both combatants, and neither man nor beast appeared to have suffered any injury. Nevertheless, the series went to the young knight who had come to the far end of the tilt yard, because his lance had found centre shield on his opponent three times. I was beginning to get the hang of the rules. I wondered if dynastic conflicts might not also be solved this way, instead of sending men to war.

"Another knight emerged from a red and white pavilion near to the edge of the lists, and immediately there were shouts and "boos" coming from the nearest rows of bleachers. 'They know this knight, and apparently they don't like him very much,' I commented, giving an appraising look across to where the knight stood, his armour a mirror of reflected sunlight.

"'Yes,' said Testagrossa, who had been quiet, up to this point, 'I don't like the looks of him very much myself.'

"'What's this?' asked Gaudin in mock dismay. 'Our gentle giant, the polite and reverend Father Testagrossa actually dislikes someone's looks?'

"'You mean someone whose looks he dislikes more than yours?' contributed Dormoy, seeing no reason not to strike a blow in Testagrossa's defence.

"While Gaudin and Dormoy were thus trading insults, the young knight, with the assistance of only one attendant mounted a heavy destrier, wheeled it briskly around and, his helmet crooked under his left arm, cantered, almost pranced his beast away from the near bleachers toward the fence where the four of us and our other companions stood. From near the dais, a herald brayed the announcement that Hugh *de Frontenac*, fourth son of Charles, *Comte de Nimes*, had entered the lists.

"'There's a braggart and an upstart for you,' said Gaudin, pointing toward the chorus of cat calls that followed the young knight's movements.

"I turned to follow the rider and caught, out of the corner of my eye, the image of my friend, Testagrossa, transfixed by the spectacle before him, eyes squinting in the direction of the proud knight, all the time clenching and releasing both his fists. It was then that I noticed what had probably so enraged the nearby spectators. The knight wore a white scarf just visible above his breast plate, clearly placed to display a token, carried at the behest of a lady. The scarf was plain, except for a large, golden brooch which joined its two halves and rested on the base of his neck, below his Adam's apple. The brooch was in the shape of a blue shield on which was emblazoned a white salamander, spouting flames from its mouth and surrounded by a golden field of its own fire.

"'How dare he presume to wear the emblem of our late king, *François*, an emblem that belongs to royalty, not to the fourth son of some provincial noble!' said Gaudin in my ear, when he saw that I, myself, was gaping at the ornament.

"I paid no attention to what Gaudin said. Instead, I turned toward Testagrossa, who was dead silent and motionless, teeth clenched and tears welling up in his eyes. At that moment, I felt strongly that it could not have been for the honour of the Valois family that my dark faced companion wept. I also knew better than to invade the privacy of this moment to press Testagrossa in so public a place. Yet I had to know what weighed so heavily on my friend's shoulders, and why these thoughts should trouble him at this moment of high entertainment.

"I turned back to the lists, where cheers and shouts of approval were rising from the bleachers like thunder from the hilltops. The crowd rose in unison to its feet as Gabriel *de Montgomery*, himself, mounted a giant sandy brown war horse. Bending down from his mount, he reached out his gauntleted hand to accept his shield, emblazoned with the red lion of Scotland, rampant on the field of amber, and deftly fastened it to the armour plate on his left arm. Next, he accepted a pro-offered helmet and placed it on his head, with a calm and steady motion, before guiding his horse, at a canter, to its position at one end of the course. Two squires simultaneously handed each knight his lance of solid oak, which the knights raised to each other in ritual salute.

"At a signal from the herald, they spurred their mounts into action. Steadily, they picked up speed as they leaned into their horses' forward momentum, their knees and thighs like iron clamps on the haunches of the animals. The field fell silent as lances lowered in aim and the two men braced for contact. Each one waited for the other to flinch and move in the saddle. An instant before contact, de Frontenac hefted his shield, only minutely, and Montgomery's lance dipped just enough to glance past the lower portion of the shield and strike his opponent squarely on the re-enforced breastplate underneath.

"The silence was broken by a sound like that of a church bell struck with a dull hammer. De Frontenac contorted, bending to form a "U" over the head of the lance and rolled, almost in slow motion from his high saddle to the swirling dust below. The crowd moaned with the weight of the blow, then cheered as a groom ran up to take the horse's reins and pull him away, lest he trample the fallen and helpless rider.

"Montgomery pulled up his horse, dismounted and bent to assist his opponent in the removal of his helmet. 'You're not ready,' he said gruffly, as if the man had just failed a spelling test. 'I told you to watch out for the dip of the lance.' Then his tone softened a bit. 'Don't worry. I hit you where you had enough padding to protect your ribs. It'll be a little sore, but nothing's broken, and you'll be fine in a couple of days.' With that, he signalled to the herald that the day's sport was over. While attendants helped the shaken de Frontenac off of the field, Montgomery lead his destrier to where a groom waited to take him to the stables of the Scottish Guards.

"At that moment, there was a howl, like a demonic laugh, coming from the unruly crowd piled up at the fence, behind which we stood. We were hemmed in as people jostled to get out of the way of what was evidently a raving madman, only a few yards behind us. Then all at once I saw and heard him, as he pushed toward the fence, his eyes, under his crushed scholar's hat, riveted to the spot where Montgomery had felled his opponent. 'The young lion, the young lion will defeat the elder on a field of single combat. He will drive a shaft through his eye, encased in a golden cage. The older will die a horrid death, and the younger will die in shame..Yes, yes, yes, he will!'

"Doctor Michel stood there in some kind of hysterical rapture, feet riveted to the ground and bony finger pointing to the spot where he most certainly thought that he could see the event he was trying to describe. Terrified faces gaped at a figure that was suddenly taller, having pulled himself out of his habitual stoop, a spectre carried on the wind, his black robe billowing, crackling as if it were being consumed by Seraphic fire.

"Dormoy fell into a kind of trance at his feet, a disciple at the Transfiguration of his master. This man, he was sure, knew the secret of the Oneness of all things, the common building blocks of which all things, including time, are made. He would follow his master to prison and to the gallows, if it came to that.

"However Testagrossa, who, in his black and evil mood, had no patience for transcendental things, shoved in between Dormoy and his dark prophet. He grabbed the old man with his two, large hairy hands, and turned him away from the place of vision. 'Go away, you old fool, before you get us all arrested!' he said through clenched teeth and with eyes seething with fury.

"With a strength belied by his frail body, Doctor Michael shook himself free. Placing both of his bony hands on Testagrossa's two shoulders, he intoned a judgement on the young theology student, for all around them to hear. 'One who is not your child will call you "father",' he said with neither mirth nor sorrow in the message.

"Gaudin laughed nervously and pulled Testagrossa away from his confrontation by grabbing the back of his brown riding cape. At the same time, he responded to my worried expression with his considered conclusion. 'For certain, a whole parish full of people in Lazio will call him "Father", if I'm not mistaken, none of whom, I hope, will have been begotten by our friend with that big head of his!'

"'Let's get out of here,' I suggested, as the crowd began to disperse. Gaudin pushed an unwilling Dormoy before him, toward the rue des Celestines, from which we had come. Dormoy moved obediently, in dull somnolence, looking behind him for a sign of his master. As I turned my head in the same direction, I caught a glimpse of the old man's robe just before it was swallowed by the encircling crowd heading toward the ancient church of the Templars.

"'What the hell was that all about?' enquired Gaudin, once they were within sight of the bridge to the *Isle de la Cité* and, beyond the island, the safety of the left bank.

"'A young lion will defeat an older one,' repeated Dormoy.

"Gaudin frowned in puzzlement. 'But young de Frontenac was bested by Montgomery, was he not? The young one did not vanquish the older one, did he?'

"'De Frontenac is a young snake, not a lion,' remarked a surly Testagrossa, breaking his silence for the first time since leaving Doctor Michel alone in the crowd.

"'Now, now, now FATHER Testagrossa,' said Gaudin, trying to lighten the mood a bit. 'My, we are touchy on the subject of this knight! Keep it up, and you'll have to go to confession before you hear Mass tomorrow morning.'

"'Oh, shut up,' retorted the Italian, in no mood for his friend's sporting banter.

"'In a golden cage?' pursued Dormoy, unable to get past the words of his spiritual master.

"'Never mind all that,' I said. 'Let's get back to our own quarter and sort this out over beer and soup,' I added pragmatically. There was no point in asking Testagrossa about his reaction in front of Gaudin. That would only end up in the two of them coming to blows that afternoon, but I was worried about my friend and I wasn't about to let the matter drop.

"When we reached *Saint-Severin*, we made for the *Ecurie*, for some sustenance, but Testagrossa, avoiding direct eye contact with any of us, excused himself and hurried off to his residence.

"Dormoy was positively manic, walking so fast that we other two could hardly keep up with him. His mind still swirled around the spectre of

Doctor Michel in ecstasy, prophesying to the dust of the tilt yard. 'A shaft in the eye, a shaft in the eye, in a golden cage,' he kept repeating, as if there were a hidden message, just for him, in these obscure words. A conversation with Dormoy would yield little on any subject but this, it seemed.

"The *Ecurie* was rapidly filling up with students and masters, thirsty and hungry at the late afternoon hour when their lectures were all concluded. The normally ebullient landlady, Marie Blanchard, spoke not one word to us three regulars, but rushed past us to clean up still more spilled beer from a table by the staircase and rescue two wooden tankards lying on the thresh covered floor, under the table.

"'She's in a foul mood for so fine a day,' remarked Gaudin after she had brushed past us, wet rag in one hand and the handles of the two tankards in the other.

"I glanced in the direction of the surely matron and drew some inferences of my own. 'Evidently, Caterina is not here today, and Madame Blanchard is providing the service in addition to supervising the kitchen staff by herself.' I considered it unlikely that she would have given the girl the day off, if they were normally this busy in the middle of the week, for the pace was chaotic. Even at the table where the three of us sat, conversation seemed to have been supplanted by three distinct monologues, none of us actually listening to what the others were saying.

"'What a fight; what poise in the saddle and control of his mount; what skill and grace with a lance!' expounded Gaudin in a continuing litany of praise for Montgomery's sporting victory over de Frontenac. He wanted to relive the experience by repeating every nuance of his master's horsemanship and skill at arms, as if it would continue happening as long as he persisted in relating its every detail. Dormoy's eyes bulged with fevered enthusiasm, as well, but without a single thought about horsemanship or skill with a lance.

"'He will pierce the older one's eye in a golden cage but end his life in shame,' paraphrased Dormoy, still searching the words, rolling them in his mouth, looking for the secret flavour of truth he was sure was hidden within them.

"Gaudin dismissed Dormoy's statement with a wave of his hand. 'Have no concern for the manner of Montgomery's death; he will live on in glory.'

"'I'm worried about Bernardo,' I said, without a thought for either Montgomery or the words of the dark prophet. 'I don't know what's come over him.'

"'You mean what's gotten into his fat head?' asked Gaudin. 'God knows! You don't suppose that he was angry because de Frontenac was humiliated by the paragon of knights, do you?'

"'On the contrary,' I observed, 'de Frontenac was apparently the focus of his anger.'

"Gaudin just shook his head. 'I don't know. It's as incomprehensible as the obsession of this Provençal dolt, over here, with what some drivelling old fool has to say about a blow to an encaged eye and the shameful death of whomever he thinks delivered the blow.'

"Dormoy stirred himself and raised a finger close to Gaudin's nose. 'He saw something, an event of great significance in the unsettled dust of that one sided battle.' It seemed to me that Dormoy had put on a look of rock solid certitude, as if he himself were a prophet of some kind.

"'I'm more concerned with what Testagrossa saw or thought he saw,' said I, determined to pursue my own subject.

"Gaudin wouldn't give up his tirade on Dormoy's idiocy. 'He actually believes that *excramentum equi* (horse shit).'

"'Very well,' I concluded. 'You try to work out the future of the *Comte de Montgomery* with Dormoy, and I will try to find out what ails Bernardo Giambelli so much that he would pass up a tankard of beer with his friends.'

"With that, we three drained our tankards and called it an evening."

Chapter 13
News From Home and
a Difficult Encounter

Journal Entry

"The next morning, I roused myself at first light, and silently, so as not to awaken Gaudin, pulled on my doublet and hose, stole quietly out into the hallway, and descended to the common room. Hunched over the enormous hearth, Mme Beber was preparing porridge for those who would be the first to greet the new day. Without looking up from the cauldron she was stirring and without so much as acknowledging that she was aware of the my presence, the old lady reached into a fold of her apron and handed me a piece of *courier* which had arrived from England the previous day.

"It was news, from my mother, already several months old, confirming the rumours that had been circulating in the taverns of Paris for some time now. Our Queen Mary had died and the new Queen Elizabeth, a Protestant, was once again redefining the boundaries of religious conformity as a measure of political loyalty. She had, so it seemed, secular interests as well, for my mother went on to say that my uncle, John de Verre, the Earl of Oxford, to whom I had sent some of my poems for criticism and, I hoped, deserved praise, had shown some of them to the new Queen.

"As learned and well read as any woman or any monarch of her time, the Queen seems to have made a point of encouraging young poets at her court or anywhere that they may have been pointed out to her. It was not clear, from my mother's letter, whether Oxford initially tried to pass off the poems as his own, but it was clear that the Queen had given them a favourable appraisal and had expressed the desire to see more from this new poet. Oxford it seems, then turned the conversation to his nephew in France, at which point the Queen expressed a desire to make my acquaintance.

"This comforted me, both on account of my pride of authorship and of my practical concern for my safety and fortune. The new regime, evidently, would continue to treat me with kind regard, unless I should give cause to be treated otherwise. It also appeared that my family's affairs were being well looked after and that there was no urgency to return, since the Queen's desire to make my acquaintance had stopped short of a summons to her presence.

"I had become so absorbed with the letter that I had forgotten why I had risen so early. I stuffed the letter into my shirt, made my excuses to the matron for passing up her morning gruel and headed out in the direction of *Sainte-Geneviève's* Abbey. I hoped to intercept my Italian friend on his way from morning Mass.

"My timing could not have been better, for I quickly spotted Testagrossa, his large mop of dark, curly, unruly hair blowing in the cross breeze as he emerged from the tall abbey gates. I had hoped that a good night's sleep and the effects of his morning devotions might have softened my friend's foul demeanour from the previous day. I soon found that this was not so, for Testagrossa at first pretended not even to have seen me and made as if he would walk by me with his eyes downcast and fixed on the stones and gravel in front of him.

"'Bernardo!' I said, putting my hand on the youth's shoulder as the distracted seminarian made to pass me.

"Testagrossa manoeuvred free from my grip and kept turning to avoid direct eye contact. 'I'm late for a lecture.'

"I moved around him in a circle so as to be able to see his face. 'What's wrong? What happened yesterday? We all seemed to be having such a good time!'

"'It's him,' said Testagrossa, without specifying to whom in particular he was referring. 'He wore her favour into the tournament. She gave him her brooch, her father's brooch.'

"I was still trying to make my friend stand still and face me. 'Who gave it to him? Who are you talking about, and how would you know from which lady a knight might have received a token of favour?'

"'De Frontenac, the snake; it was him. He's the one who took it from her.' The Italian's story came spilling out, one incoherent detail after another.

"'De Frontenac took it from whom?' I pursued, 'and I thought a lady gives a token of favour. No knight of honour would wear a favour he had stolen from some lady!'

"'He has no honour. He tricked her,' insisted Testagrossa, getting angrier by the minute, as he repeated the story. 'He charmed her and seduced her into giving it to him! She's innocent. She doesn't know anything about the world, about men like him!'

"I tried to interject reason in the midst of my friend's tirade of rage and conjecture. 'And do you know the world, my seminarian friend? Have you, yourself, navigated the winding alleys on the dark side of this fallen world?'

"'I know what's right and fitting and appropriate for a girl of her station,' continued Testagrossa with stubborn insistence. 'I gave her brotherly, priestly advice. I know what men like him do with girls like her. They take their most precious possession, their innocence, and they move on to the next conquest, that's what they do.'

"I took my friend by the arm and gently moved him from the path, where we could speak quietly. 'Why don't you have a pint and some bread with me and tell me how all this happened?' I tried to make my voice as soothing as possible.

"'No, I have to get to Father Eusebius and I can't stay and chat,' answered Testagrossa with some impatience. 'I've already said too much anyway. Thank you for your concern, Henry, but there's no point in trying to make me look at this differently.'

"Testagrossa hastened down the street without bothering to take his leave, still angry, still capable of some as yet undetermined desperate action. Nevertheless, I had acquired some insight into my friend's state of mind. Although Testagrossa protectively avoided using her name, I concluded that the young lady in question must be Caterina from the *Ecurie*. Had I not seen them in frequent conversation ever since that evening, now almost two years ago, when I had first met them both?

"Testagrossa was always a bit rigid in his application of moral principles, and he was incorrigibly chivalrous and protective, in regard to women and children. I had always attributed this strict social conservatism to my friend's Italian upbringing, a Latin, Mediterranean heritage, but, to me the vehemence with which he sought to protect Caterina seemed to have gone well beyond such a cultural influence. This was not a matter of a theoretical principle. Rather, it was deeply personal and important to Testagrossa in ways that probably he, himself, did not begin to understand.

"I thought about all this on my way back to the room I shared with Gaudin on rue St Victor. I knew I couldn't discuss Testagrossa's situation with Gaudin, so I told him, instead, about the letter from England, and the favourable reception my poems had received from the Queen, herself.

"'Damn that Oxford,' volunteered Gaudin, who chose the darker side of the story over the prospect of offering genuine praise for my work. 'It would greatly please me to go with you to England and pound this Oxford's head with the hilt of my sword.' It seemed to me that Gaudin's language had undergone a sudden, more bellicose alteration to mimic his concept of high chivalric discourse.

"'This is hardly a matter of such moment that it would necessitate our crossing the channel to right it,' I replied, rendering my own version of the high speech, an affectation which Gaudin either didn't notice or chose to ignore.

"'Still, you deserve credit for what you write,' argued Gaudin, coming back down to the more comfortable level of ordinary speech.

"'I hardly think people will be quoting my lines hundreds of years from now and crediting someone else with them, do you?' I smiled at the absurdity of the idea.

"Gaudin smiled, too, and, changing the subject, asked me: 'How is our fat-headed friend doing? Gotten over his fit of distemper and busy praying again, I suppose.'

"I really didn't want to share my suspicions about what was ailing Testagrossa, so I simply shrugged and replied: 'Not exactly.' Wishing to deflect the conversation from the subject of our Italian friend, I asked: 'Did you make any headway with diverting the enraptured disciple?'

"'Not really,' said Gaudin, his hands opening in an admission of defeat. 'I think you should try to decode his alchemy books with him. You're a scholar and, besides, you're the only one of us with any chance of getting him to open up.'

"'Maybe I'll just go to the Celestines with him, but there's another piece of business I have to attend to first,' I said, without elaborating.

"Gaudin seemed to have lost interest in the matter. 'As you wish. I'm not at all convinced that it will do any good, anyway.'

"I took this as a dismissal and went out by myself, determined to have lunch and some elucidating conversation at *L'Ecurie*.

Chapter 14
Another Difficult Conversation

"**S**ince it was too early in the day for the after-lecture crowd to have congregated *en masse* at their favourite haunt, I had no trouble finding a quiet corner table out of the direct line of sight from the staircase. I knew that I had little skill in witty conversation with women, but the prospect of a serious discussion, to which the lady was not likely to be receptive, was enough to make the palms of my hands perspire profusely. 'This is for Testagrossa,' I said to myself, and braced myself for the encounter.

"After what seemed like an interminable wait, Caterina appeared at my table, wooden mug in hand and offering me a pleasant smile. 'I see you are alone today, Signor Howard. Will Bernardo and his other friends be meeting you here?' She was not rushed, today, so she allowed herself a few pleasantries, while placing the tankard in front of me. I grasped the beer with both hands, so that I could keep them still while I attempted to engage the waitress in conversation.

"'No,' I said, 'I am having my lunch alone today, but I hope you will not think it impertinent if I ask for a word with you – about Testagrossa – if you are not too busy at this moment.'

"'Please don't call him that in front of me! His name is Bernardo, and it pains me when I see the other students make fun of him like that.'

"'Forgive me,' I said, 'I intended no ridicule or disrespect. On the contrary, I must speak to you because I am worried about his state of mind, of late. He is my friend, too, you know,' I added, hoping to establish a bond with the girl on that basis.

"Caterina's look softened, as she noted the evident concern in my eyes. 'I know. Bernardo often speaks about you with genuine affection. You are the only one who doesn't laugh at him.'

"'He hasn't been laughing very much lately, either,' I replied, steering the conversation back to Testagrossa. 'He is concerned about someone, someone who means a great deal to him, someone he thinks might be in danger of making a grave mistake.'

"Caterina would not risk sitting down with a customer and being caught at it by Mme. Blanchard, but there was no one else to be served, at the moment, and she stood by the table, bereft of her usual poise and confident composure. 'Has he told you who this person is?' she asked, with a look on her face that belied the answer.

"'No, he didn't,' said I, warming to my task. 'He thinks too highly of this person's reputation to betray her identity, even to a good friend, but he did tell me about a brooch, one I, myself, saw being worn as a token by a young knight. The brooch was azure, with a white salamander on a field of golden fire.'

"'Yes,' she said, looking, for the first time, lost and frightened. 'That is my brooch, a gift my father received from the old King himself.'

"I lowered my voice trying to sound as non-judgemental as possible. 'I would consider such a gift to have been a treasure worth keeping, if not for the sake of its intrinsic value, then because it had belonged to your father.'

"'I know it was a foolish thing, but it was all I could do to make amends for having cruelly sent him away!'

"I furrowed my brow in puzzlement. 'You sent him away?'

"'Yes, because Bernardo convinced me that this is what I should do.' She had lost her reserve and clearly wanted to blurt out everything that troubled and confounded her mind. Nevertheless, she paused and, seeming to turn away, busied herself with wiping the adjacent table with a damp cloth which she took from the apron string around her waist.

"I knew that Caterina had to continue to look busy, to avoid being scolded by the ever watchful Mme. Blanchard. Scrubbing tables with a rag also help her work off some of her nervousness and embarrassment.

"'We'd better start at the beginning.' As gently as I could, I pursued my line of questioning in the hope of picking up the missing pieces of the story. 'How did you make the acquaintance of this knight, in the first place?'

"'It started about four months ago, on my day off. I took some laundry that my mother had done for the family of the *Comtesse de Nimes*, who were staying at the *Louvre*. On my way through the corridors, heading back to the servants' entrance, I encountered Hugh de Frontenac, who had just come from his father's apartments.

"'He was tall and handsome and straight as a Roman statue, with fair hair and the ruddy complexion of a man who spends much time in sport and outdoor pleasures. He bowed gallantly, in the manner of one who was not disposed to treat me like a servant. In a rather pleasant tone, he asked me my business in these apartments, and I told him, with no little embarrassment, that I was delivering laundered and pressed garments to the *Comtesse*. He tried to put me at my ease and described himself as a modern man who judged others more by their accomplishments than by the length of their pedigree.

"'We spoke of my father and his paintings at Fontainebleau, about which the old King François had lavished so much praise. He said that he had been to Fontainebleau and seen the magnificent banquet hall which my father worked on for three years. He made me feel what I haven't felt in I can't remember how long – I felt pride in having been my father's daughter.'

"I spoke softly and soothingly, the better to encourage her to continue. 'And so, you continued to see him?'

"'Yes.' Caterina sounded actually apologetic.. 'We would meet in the gardens of Notre Dame or at Les Celestines, and we would walk and talk.'

"'...in secret?' I suggested.

"'Oh no' replied Caterina hastily, 'I told my mother where I was going, and we always met in public places, with his pages and retainers around us.'

"'You also told Testa...I mean, Bernardo?'

"She nodded and then turned her face toward the table she was scrubbing for the seventh time with the same beer stained dish towel. 'He was FURIOUS with me!' She pushed so hard with the dirty cloth, I thought she might make a hole in the oak table. 'He told me there was only one thing that I could expect from a lusty, high born climber, like Hugh, and I was to pay no attention to any pledges of love and honour that he may have offered me. They are all tricks and perjury!' She sniffed back a tendency to cry, determined to maintain her composure in front of anyone who might report her behaviour back to Testagrossa.

"I was careful not to take sides. 'He was convinced that de Frontenac would try to take advantage of you?'

"'But he didn't,' protested the now uncontrollably tearful Caterina. 'He was gentle, and he always treated me with such kindness, but Bernardo would not hear a word in his defence. He kept on saying that Hugh would not rest until he had had his way with me, and then he would move on to another girl.'

"'That is his reputation,' I commented.

"A flash of anger covered Caterina's face. 'One's reputation can be concocted by such mean and spiteful people.'

"'Yes, and a bad reputation, deserved or undeserved, can shipwreck a person's whole life!' I realised, even as I said the words, how pompous and Testagrossa-like I sounded.

"'I have more than ugly gossip to consider,' added Caterina, 'I have my mother's happiness and security to think of.'

"I turned in my seat to look directly at the weeping and, at the same time, defiant girl. This was a new twist to the story. 'What does your mother have to do with this?'

"'Do you think my mother was meant to be washing other people's clothes? Do you think she can go on taking in laundry forever? If Hugh gets us re-introduced at court, as genteel folk, then my mother can go back to the way we lived at Fontainebleau. She can spend her old age in modest comfort.'

"Despite myself, I must have sounded incredulous. 'You're doing this for your mother? Do you love de Frontenac and do you believe that he loves you?'

"'I can only believe what he tells me, and that he wants to be with me. I don't know if this is enough to secure our future, but I feel I must try,' declared Caterina with a look that spoke more of grim determination than it did of fondness. 'But Bernardo did not go along with my reasoning. He said that in the end, both my mother and I would be irreparably damaged by this young gallant, and that my hopes for a secure future lay with someone of my own class and rank. "Even if he does love you, in the end, he must marry for reasons of family and property, not for reasons of the heart," he told me.'

"'So, he convinced you to break it off?' I pursued.

"'Yes, he and I spoke here one night, and I agreed to do so. Then he seemed happy and relieved, and he became his old charming self. He called me his little sparrow and talked to me so gently, as he always used to do.'

"'He called you his "sparrow"?' I furrowed my brow, as if the story had taken yet another twist. I didn't say anything for several long moments, then I must have looked as if I had come to some kind of conclusion. I brought the subject back to de Frontenac. 'So, you kept your word to Bernardo and you broke it off with de Frontenac, but then you gave him your brooch?'

"'Yes, yes, I had to, don't you see? My mother was disappointed in me. I could tell, even though she didn't say anything. I had dashed her chances of ever returning to her former station, and I saw her looking OLD, for the very first time. I passed a note to one of Hugh's servants, saying that I wanted to see him again. The next day, the servant found me in the market place and delivered his master's reply. Hugh would see me again, but I must give him the brooch, for him to wear as a favour in the next tournament. He said he required a token of my earnest sincerity, proof that I would treat him seriously and not toy with his affections.'

"My reaction was pensive. 'Naturally, you didn't tell Bernardo that you were seeing him again.'

"'I couldn't, not after having given him my word that I would end it.' Caterina was pleading, and the tears and sniffles came flooding back.

"'That would explain his surprise and anger at the joust,' I concluded.

"I now understood the problem, but no solution came readily to mind. 'I think you need to be honest with our friend. You need to talk to Bernardo and tell him what you told me. He'll get angry, but let him. If I know anything about my friend, I know that he could never hurt someone he loves, and he'll prove with every angry word how much he truly loves you.'

"Caterina looked frantic now. She was ringing the wet rag in her hand as if she wanted to remove every trace of what was in it. 'How can he love me, after I have broken my word to him?'

"'Trust him. He can forgive anything except your turning away from him in fear. You need a friend, and right now, he's the best one you've got.'

"'Bernardo is lucky to have a friend like you,' Caterina said. 'I'm really grateful for your kind words, but I still don't know what I shall do!'

"'Be a friend to Bernardo. He needs your friendship, and he needs you to tell him that you understand how he feels. Do you think you can understand that big old fool?'

"Caterina looked as if she, too, had reached a decision. 'Yes, I think I can. I think I do.'

"She went back to the kitchen, crying, I was sure, not for the first time in recent weeks. I had no idea whether I had helped or hindered the situation today, nor did I know what I could do, at this juncture, to be of some comfort to them. I can only note my misgivings in this journal.

"Sometimes, when we interfere with the best of intentions in the course of events, we only succeed in making them worse. Perhaps it's best to let these matters take their course."

Chapter 15
Another Journey
to the Right Bank

Journal Entry

"Feeling powerless to do more for my friend, Testagrossa, or for Caterina, and unwilling to share my insights with Gaudin, who would be sure to exacerbate the situation by making sport of the love-sick seminarian, I arranged to meet with Dormoy, convinced that another point of view could do no harm.

"Dormoy had been keeping mostly to himself since the joust and its apocalyptic aftermath, and when I first caught sight of him at the table that afternoon, in Cutter's tavern, I almost failed, at first, to recognise him. The familiar tankard of ale was there, sure enough, clutched in his right fist, held tightly enough for his knuckles to show white around the handle, but his characteristic slouch and injured facial expression were replaced by an essence of something I could not, initially, fathom. His clothes, too, looked different, not the careless country cut and light colours that bespoke his Provençal origins, but the sombre robe and hat of an apothecary or an alchemist.

"He had stopped attending lectures and withdrawn from all but the most essential social pastimes. He said that he was immersed in independent studies and was seeking out only those masters who were willing to lead their students down to the essential elements and up to the prognosticating stars. Alchemy and astrology, he said, opened the doors to truths that philosophy and theology, logic and rhetoric, had firmly closed to him and to others who were intimidated by the academic establishment. With arcane knowledge and forbidden arts, he could know the future, remix the elements of this world, remake his destiny and even cheat death, for himself and, more importantly, for those who were closest to him.

"In the fever of his new faith, he seemed to have even forgotten his friends, except for me, who did not take gratuitous pleasure in belittling his beliefs or making sport at his expense. If there was to be a new order for those in possession of the knowledge of the ages, Dormoy thought that I, of all people, ought to have a place of honour therein, among wise and poetic souls.

"I thought I might build on this trust and try to re-establish Dormoy's contact with the real world. I proposed that we complete our outing to the library of the Celestines, the outing that had been cut short by the fateful events at the jousting pitch. Perhaps it was possible to reunite Dormoy with the race of mortals he had left behind to follow the dark Doctor Michel.

"On the day of our expedition to the Celestines, we had arranged to meet at a tavern called the *Bois d'Oré*, off of the St Michel not far from the bridge that connected the left bank to *l'Isle de la Cité*, from which we could cross, via another bridge, to the right bank.

"I saw Dormoy long before the latter deigned to take notice of me, or anyone else, for that matter. He was looking intently at the stone facing behind my head, his eyes wide and fixed, his neck, shoulders and arms held as if tensed, prepared to lunge forward at any moment, but the moment never came. He appeared to me in a state of agitated expectation, as if he were just about to catch sight of something that he was never quite able to see.

"I waited until the fog of Dormoy's trance looked to have somewhat dissipated, before I moved closer to the table of the young astrologer and raised my hand in greeting. Dormoy eyed me with suspicion, at first, seeming to brace himself for more of the ridicule that his change in appearance had provoked among his other acquaintances. Seeing that my questioning look betrayed genuine concern, he relaxed his vigilance, and the cloud-like mask that had covered his visage began to dissolve.

"'I may seem strange to you,' said Dormoy, 'but it was my old self, morose and taciturn, which was alien to my true character. This is the REAL Claude Dormoy, the man of purpose hidden behind whatever I was until now. Doctor Michel showed me who I am and where I have kept myself hidden, all these years.'

"Dormoy didn't just look different; his speech was different, too, more like that of someone who means more than he says. I always loved to imitate people's speech patterns, not to mock them but because I thought it was like another feature of the face, differentiating each of us from one another. I continued my friend's train of thought, hoping Dormoy would perceive this as a kind of empathy. '...and you suppose that it was Doctor Michel who set you free from your former self?'

"'He just led me to the threshold. It was I who chose to cross it,' said the young alchemist with a look of self-approbation that was so unlike the Dormoy I thought I knew.

"'Actually, those sombre shades suite you better than the bright hues of Provence ever did, but it's you and not your clothes that I find most altered.'

"'So it is with all men,' said Dormoy, sounding to me more like Testagrossa than himself. 'We gaze into the limpid pool of our life's own misery and we either bemoan what we see or we remake the image, which is our very self, in a manner that befits our proper destiny.'

"'So then, you see,' I continued, in the same vein, 'not what you are but what you can or will be.'

"At these words, a burning intensity lit Dormoy's eyes. 'Precisely, I think, sometimes, I can see the future as clearly as I can see the past.'

"'It is precisely the future that I have come to discuss, neither yours nor mine, for the moment, but rather, that of our friend, Testagrossa. He is greatly troubled, of late, neither about his past nor his intended future. I am afraid that it is with the present that he is engaged in such tortuous conflict, a conflict he must resolve, if he is to have any future happiness at all.'

"'He is conflicted about the present?' Dormoy scowled at the idea.

"'Indeed he is. He has no idea how to respond to being in love.'

"'Ah, *Amor vincit omnes*" ("Love conquers all"),' quoted Dormoy, looking relieved at the thought.

"'The problem is: he doesn't know he is in love, so he can't understand why he feels or acts the way he does.'

"'Testagrossa can't understand the present, but I'm the fool because I understand the future!'

"'For God's sake, man, this isn't about you. Testagrossa's in trouble, and I want to know what we can do to help!'

"'It's always like this.' Dormoy suddenly had re-assumed both his old defeated, hang-dog face and his old diction. 'Even Doctor Michel seems more interested in my friends than he is in me. I guess I'm not such a valuable disciple after all! He's constantly jabbering about you, about how you are destined to be rattling pikes around the world, when you have reached your full maturity.'

"'Pikes? Is he mad? If he sees things the way he claims, he must know that my brother is the soldier of the family, not me!'

"'I have no idea what he means, but he says that people will remember you, "the rattler of pikes" long after the soldiers and statesmen of this century will have been dead and forgotten.'

"'...and what has your famous Doctor Michel got to say about our friend Testagrossa?'

"'He keeps repeating the same thing over and over about his priesthood: that he will be called 'Father', and so he will. He even raves on about Gaudin, who apparently is to follow a Scotsman to a fortress in the north, where he will give his life in the cause of the King of Navarre, always this King of Navarre.'

"I wearily lowered my head into both of my outstretched hands. 'None of this is particularly helpful, unless rattling a pike can shake some sense into our Italian friend's head, I suppose.'

"'Maybe the esoteric books will give us a clue.' Clearly, Dormoy was still hoping that we would adhere to the original purpose of our meeting.

"'Yes, by all means. Let's go on to the Celestine library and see if there is any ancient riddle to help us solve this modern one.'

"Leaving our tankards of beer behind, we ventured across the two bridges that joined them to the island and the right bank of the river. As we made our way up broad new carriage ways, turning east in the direction of the Celestine convent and the residence of *Les Tournelles*, we became aware that Dormoy's robes were catching more than one suspicious glare from the soldiers in the *Guise* livery who lounged about their posts at the major crossroads. Nevertheless, we managed to arrive unmolested at the great southern gate of the convent, the portal to the massive library of which the Celestine monks were the proprietors.

"Dormoy strode into the place like a minister of state, robes swishing on the stone floors, his eyes spanning this way and that, until he spied a suitably nervous looking young novice who was guiding visitors to the priory that day. Carelessly waving Brother Lawrence' letter of introduction, which he had pulled from the folds of his academic gown, Dormoy commanded the boy to conduct us, with all due haste, to the brother librarian, on urgent business for the Abbey of *Sainte-Geneviève*. The awe struck boy promptly guided the both of us, as if we were ecclesiastical dignitaries, straight to the librarian's office, where he handed over the letter, with its raised seal of red wax. Then, bowing deeply, first to the librarian and then to the two of us (much to my amusement), he hastily took his leave.

"The librarian, Brother Sixtus, a tall and straight backed man of greying and wrinkled aspect, was not so easily impressed. From his vantage point of clear academic superiority, he was disposed to treat us both with the passive but palpable force of his contempt.

"Dormoy asked for a volume that was called, in Latin, *Secretum Secretorum*, or the book of the Secret of Secrets, a translation of a 10th century Arabic text that was a kind of a compendium of ancient wisdom about politics, ethics, physiognomy, astrology, alchemy, sorcery and medicine. Brother Sixtus pronounced the title as if it were vomit in his mouth. He turned his irritated scowl on the no longer so self-confident Dormoy, who was fidgeting with the full sleeves of his gown. The deflated youth forced himself to nod in acquiescence.

"Now ready for his next victim, the tall monk turned to me, his jaw set to challenge any credentials I might bethink myself to possess. 'What shall I procure for you, young man?' The question fell from Brother Sixtus's inquisitorial lips down to me in the same way that a school master's interrogation assaults a recalcitrant pupil.

"'I would like to see what the ancients had to say about love,' I replied, trying not to let the self-important librarian intimidate me.

"'*De Amore!*' said the librarian while his lip curled in a sneer only slightly less contemptuous than the one he had for the Secret of Secrets. 'I thought all young people imagine that they, themselves, invented love. Well, Aristotle, of course has said that Love is composed of a single soul inhabiting two bodies, but if it's advice you want, you'd best go to Ovid for his treatment of the *Ars Amatoria* (The Art of Love). Still, the Italian romances are said to best capture the essence and passion of what the Greeks called "*eros*". Do you read Italian?'

"'No, but I know someone who does.' I thought of my friend without the slightest note of optimism.

"'Pity,' replied the librarian, 'I happen to have a tale called *Giulietta e Romeo*, by this fellow, Matteo Bandello, a very popular work among those who can read the vernacular. As a matter of fact, I had an enterprising young man in here only last week, a young master named François *de Belleforest*. He said he was working on a French translation of the Bandello *contes*. You don't, by any chance, know the fellow?'

"I perked up at the mention of the name. 'Actually, I attended one of his lectures, on the *Gesta Danorum* (Tales of the Danes) *of Saxo Grammaticus*.'

"'Fascinating collection of stories, the *Gesta Danorum*, love, intrigue, murder, revenge...'

"'Revenge... what an edifying Christian sentiment for a monk's spiritual reading.' Dormoy permitted himself the observation, seeming to have regained his new confidence.

"'Better than magic and necromancy,' replied the brother librarian with an irritated twist of his thin lips.

"'I think I'll take a look at Ovid's *Ars Amatoria*,' I said, hoping to forestall another sardonic barb from Brother Sixtus, directed at my friend,' ...and the *Saxo Grammaticus*,' I added.

"Brother Sixtus nodded to a passing assistant who conducted us to a visitors' reading room, cramped and poorly lit. We were left to read by candlelight, while perched on stools facing each other at either end of a small table.

"I quickly decided that Ovid's advice to lovers was more reminiscent of a lecherous old uncle or nurse than the serious counsel of a wise teacher.

Finding myself at the end of yet another blind alley, I reached for the volume of *Saxo Grammaticus*. I recalled something that had captured my interest in the course of Belleforest's lecture, and, leafing through the book, I found a certain tale, '*Vita Amlethi*,' which suited my dark and melancholy mood. So here was a tale of a young man whose father, like mine, had been murdered for political gain. Do you suppose that Amleth shared with me both anger and relief, both sadness and guilt in the face of events against which I seemed unable or unwilling to take any action?

"As I paused to mouth the strange sounding Scandinavian names from a cold and misty past, I glanced across the table to where Dormoy was also mumbling scarcely intelligible arcane Latin words and phrases in an attempt to extract the magical content of these ancient incantations. Magic and mystery dangled the promise of an answer, while tantalizingly masking its meaning in a foggy cloak of obscurity. They were, at best, duplicitous and equivocal; at worst, false and illusory. I had had enough.

"Dormoy did not want to stop reading. He was certain that everything would become clear to him, if he would only read on another five or ten minutes, but I insisted on terminating our exercise and indicated to the librarian's assistant that we were prepared to return our books. We were met at the other side of the reading room door by a burley looking brother with a set of ponderous keys jingling from his cincture. The heavy set brother neither identified himself nor exchanged any pleasantries. He walked with us wordlessly to the main door, at which point he opened his mouth, for the one and only time, to tell us to go with God.

"The outside air was a welcome change, after the stale, shadowy closet where we had been confined with our reading, and I, for one, welcomed the noise and bustle that greeted us, once we had passed through the convent's ponderous oaken doors. People seemed to be even more boisterous than usual, the commotion coming from the direction of the jousting field at *Les Tournelles*. The two of us agreed that a slight detour to the place where Dormoy had experienced his epiphany and where Testagrossa had seen his great rival wearing his lady's favour into combat, would be just the thing for both of our recent preoccupations.

"The crowds seemed to be milling aimlessly, as there were no combats that day. Instead, most of the field was taken up by workmen, engaged either in levelling the ground and filling in holes or shovelling prodigious quantities of horse droppings into buckets. The excrement was then hauled, by the youngest and lowliest among them, to a kind of pit or long trench which had been dug for this purpose, earlier in the day.

"On the side closest to the palace, other workers were assembling a large, new, covered viewing stand, intended for royal spectators as well as the highest of the well born and wealthy. On the other end of the field, additional rickety bleachers were being hastily erected, for spectators of lesser station. A few young squires were leading some of the younger, more skittish chargers by the bridle in careful circles around the field to familiarise them with the dips and elevations of the ground: the turns, the distances and the general layout of the field.

"Suddenly, I spotted my room-mate, Gaudin, leading a grey and chocolate stallion onto the pitch. Gaudin was cursing at the beast for constantly rearing its powerful neck. At the same time, he was coaxing the creature forward in the general direction of the fence at which we stood, observing.

"Gaudin had been spending little time in our room, of late, and even less time at lectures or libraries, since he had announced his decision to join the company of Gabriel, *Comte de Montgomery*, to be in the service of a man of valour. As surely as Dormoy had fallen in as a disciple of Doctor Michel, Gaudin had committed himself, in body and in heart, to his illustrious captain for the pursuit of glory, as becomes a man of courage and honour. No more the juvenile prankster, he now enjoyed a calling to high seriousness and hard work – not excluding the hauling of horse manure from the field – in the eager pursuit of glory. I wasn't sure if Gaudin's new friends in the service of the Captain would replace his old academic fellows, but I was at least reassured that the aspiring fighter could still recognise Dormoy and me in a crowd, from a distance.

"'Good to see you, my fine fellows,' Gaudin called out while wrestling with the bridle of the beast he had in tow. He moved closer to the fence in a series of circular diversions and recoveries caused by the animal's desire to go the other way, finally coming to rest at a distance where conversation was possible. 'So, what news from the haunts of the Latin speakers?'

"I wanted to say something about Testagrossa and Caterina, but I thought better of it. Dormoy, reluctant to give Gaudin another pretext for making fun of his master, likewise hesitated to speak of what was foremost on his mind. Gaudin took our blank stares for tell-tale signs of the idleness with which he had increasing come to regard his former academic life. His story, therefore, was undoubtedly of much greater interest.

"'The days pass very quickly here,' continued Gaudin, his eyes wide with excitement, his speech uncharacteristically fast and devoid of his customary ironic detachment. 'There's so much to do and so much to learn from the Captain. Why, there's a whole new vocabulary to acquire, not only about the knights' battle attire but about what the horses wear, as well.'

"I made a pointing motion with my head in the general direction over Gaudin's shoulder. 'What preparations do the builders make?'

"'A marriage has been concluded between the King's daughter and that persistent pain in the ass, Philip of Spain, to seal a treaty of lasting peace between them. So we will have a grand combat, starting in two days, to celebrate peace, and the cracking of heads to mark and seal the bonds of matrimony.'

"I smiled at the irony. 'How fitting!'

"'And my captain, the *Comte de Montgomery*, will fight with only his most advanced knights in the lists.'

"I was interested, but perhaps not for the same reason as Gaudin. 'Will that young fellow we saw last time be among them? I think his name was de Frontenac.'

"'Most likely,' admitted Gaudin without pleasure. 'The Captain, my master, has been grilling him almost daily about his technique and concentration. Personally, I don't think he's much with a lance, but he is well enough connected to make it worth the Captain's while to train him. I don't really think the captain likes him very much, for all that.'

"'I don't suggest you discuss that particular fellow with our heavy set Italian friend, if you know what's good for you,...if you even deign to dine with us again.' I suppose that my face was uncharacteristically grim, clearly not receptive to any attempts at derisive humour.

"'Do you know how long a walk it is between the Scottish armoury and our old haunts? Do you know how busy they keep me, between oiling tackle and hauling horse shit for the captain? The road to glory is mired in the muddy ruts of the artillery wagon wheels and trails of animal droppings, you know,' protested Gaudin, his defensive head held high in search of his lost dignity.

"'And Howard, here, must endure Mme. Beber's complaints and suppositions about why you don't come home at night. You're reputed to have tarried with every barmaid on the St Germain,' added Dormoy. He was evidently enjoying the opportunity to tease the teaser.

"'Very well, then, what about tonight, at the *Ecurie*? I think I can escape from shovelling duty at the shit pile long enough to take a meal together with some old friends.'

"The mention of *L'Ecurie* immediate brought me back to my major preoccupation. 'Maybe Father Testagrossa will be there to see his old friends, and we can restore his spirits with a good dosage of fellowship.'

"'It's worth a try,' said Dormoy, thinking of his master's words about Testagrossa's being called 'Father' by people other than his offspring.

"'And the Captain would surely give me a night off to help an old friend, now that almost everything is ready,' added Gaudin with what sounded to me like real interest in the endeavour.

"So, we parted, with the promise to meet for supper and to band together in the cause of helping our tormented friend."

Dan Scannell

Chapter 16
Where Matters take
a Turn for Testagrossa

Journal Entry

"I was in a hurry, intending to come between the tactless Gaudin and the hypersensitive Testagrossa, if, indeed, the increasingly unpredictable Italian decided to show up. I spun down the spiral stairs to the perpetually shaded cave with its ancient beams, wooden tables and sputtering candles. After a moment, I spotted only Dormoy, wearing his old worried and confused face, instead of the new, self-assured, alchemist's one. From where he was seated, towards the rear, Dormoy had contorted his body into a half turn, the better to peer at the ceiling of the cave, furthest from the staircase, into which a small opening had been hewn, to permit the ventilation of air to the outside.

"Through the opening, he could distinctly hear voices that grew louder and more excited by the minute. So loud had the voices become, that they drowned out the rumble of wagon wheels and the cat calls of street urchins with which they had been in competition. As I approached and listened, too, it became clear that the voices were one male and one female, and that they were speaking Italian. I gave my friend a furtive look and pointed, my finger shooting up between our faces, at the gaping hole behind them. Before listening to any more of the exchange and without a word to Dormoy, I spun around and bounded back up the spiral staircase, from whence I had just come.

"Once I had attained the ground floor, I turned, not left, toward the door, but right, into the kitchen. With one foot committed, I halted and turned, having caught sight of my friend, Gaudin, out of the corner of my eye, just then entering the door. Wordlessly, I motioned to my friend to continue on below, while I resumed my path into the kitchen.

"Such was my stride and the determined expression I no-doubt wore, that no one tried to stop me, before I reached and push open the heavy door of the service entrance. Once through the door, I found himself in the open early evening air, my foot partially covering the vent from the cave, below.

"After I had shut out the rectangle of light that had flooded into the alley behind me, I stepped into the arms of the night. On the opposite corner, almost totally obscured in the approaching darkness, except for the first dim illumination of a crescent moon, I spied two bent figures, under a torn awning in the gathering gloom. I was unable to make out their faces, although they could not have been more than 20 feet from where I stood. Nevertheless, I had no trouble identifying the lumbering bear-like form of Testagrossa and the slim, diminutive silhouette of Caterina.

"They took no notice, when the restaurant service entrance door had swung open, and now that I was standing concealed in the shadow of the restaurant building, it was as if both they and I were still alone. Although I could not understand all of their words, I could not mistake the desperation and frustration of their gesticulating arms and crouching body language. I heard the word, 'bambino' and a horrible premonition seized me. Suddenly, they turned, startled by the sound of a familiar voice which had simply said the name: 'Bernardo'.

"Alarm melted into surprise, as I stepped out of the building's shadow and stood at their side, under the awning. To their immense relief, it was not the heavy set dish washer or Marie's husband; it was what they desperately feared and needed: a friend.

"'Henri,' came the pleading sound, bursting from Caterina's lips. I could see her raised face, cheeks streaked with tears. 'I'm sorry. I'm so, so sorry!'

"'It's not your fault,' said Testagrossa, having regained some of his composure. 'It is that recreant *chevalier* who must be made to pay for this!'

"Although certain that I already knew the answer, I posed the question: 'Will someone please tell me what has happened?' They both looked shameful, but it was Caterina who raised her head to speak.

"'I promised Bernardo that I would break it off with him – with Hugh – and I meant to, I wanted to. I returned his gifts and told his servant that the dictates of my honour, my modesty and my heart had so prevailed that I determined thus and begged his gentleness to concur withal.

"'I felt relieved, but when I returned to our lodgings, my mother was in a torrent of tears, hot with pity and rage. She called me selfish and petty and faithless in my duty to a mother who had suffered long and back breaking humiliation to keep me in clothes and some semblance of genteel prospects. "And what am I to do without title or means? Have you given a thought to my old age, abandoned by your father, abandoned by fortune, fallen from a cottage and modest household to the chambers of a common washer woman? At least with *Monsieur* de Frontenac there was a chance that we would be favoured with court lodgings – even a gentleman's mistress and her train are afforded these. Now what shall we do, whom shall you marry – the son of a butcher or stone mason? After all I have sacrificed for you, the least you could do is think, THINK of me!" She raved and wept until I agreed to send to his servant to beg for an audience.'

"'And what of your honour, your modesty and your word to ME,' asked the wounded and desperate Testagrossa.

"All that Caterina could manage were a series of shaking sobs in between rasping intakes of breath.

"I thought about the other side of the triangle. 'And for de Frontenac you felt...?'

"'Nothing, and when I saw him next he only confirmed what I already knew, that he was too passionately in love with himself to seek anything but self-affirmation from any other person.'

"I hated to ask what I knew was coming next. 'Did he take you back on stricter terms, did his pride demand some sort of satisfaction?'

"'His wounded pride demanded subjugation to his great will. Gone was the polite banter and play of courtship. Teeth bared, he demanded that I unmask my body to him and give myself to him, right then and there, in what I swear was more like revenge than love.'

"'That base and recreant son of a mongrel BITCH,' exploded Testagrossa while hot tears of rage seared his puffy cheeks. His fists, raised helplessly to the gathering mists of night, were clenched white at the knuckles.

"Caterina's eyes flashed in sudden anger, as if it were happening to her right then and there. 'I turned from him, feeling nothing but loathing and disgust. I've never felt so angry, so murderously angry before. I told him "NO" and swung my right arm around, close fisted. I think I hit him in the face, because he stepped back momentarily, but then he came at me. He hit me twice, and when I fell, he dragged me by my hair to a near-by couch. When I made to squirm away he grabbed both my hands with one of his, and with the other he pulled a knife from his belt and held to my throat. Then he released my hands. Without taking his eyes from my throat and his knife, he picked up a goblet from the small round table that was in front of the couch. I also caught a glimpse of an open beaker lying on its side at the edge of the table.

"'Drink,' he said, through clenched teeth. I remembered my hands and moved to push the cup away, but he was too quick for me. He angrily evaded my hands and pressed the rim of the cup to my lips. I felt the liquid dripping from my chin onto my neck. He poured until it filled my throat and I swallowed without meaning to. Then I could no longer feel my limbs, as if I were trapped in a kind of paralysis. I felt slimy, sticky hands all over me. As if I were a spectator in a nightmare, I watched as he jammed his fullness in me, again and again...and although I tried, I could neither move nor speak.' Caterina's helpless anger gave way to racking sobs and uncontrollable tears.

"I put an arm around each of them and made 'shushing' sounds, in a helpless attempt to sooth them. 'It was rape, not love, and the shame, Caterina, is not yours to bear, but his.'

"'What I have to bear is, I hope, longer lived than shame. My monthly course of blood has stopped. I'm daily sick at the very smell of morning porridge. I am carrying his child!'

"In the muted pause that ensued, I noted that Testagrossa moved his hand ever so slightly until it covered her trembling one. His large, puffy paw softly caressed her thin, filament like fingers and the back of her chilled hand, warming and soothing the pain in rising waves that radiated to her bosom. They lingered thus a long moment, but they never once permitted their averted eyes to make contact.

"'How long?' I asked, finally breaking the silence.

"'A month,' said Testagrossa, as if the question had been addressed to him. 'It was one of the nights she didn't show up for work and Mme Blanchard was in a particularly surly mood.'

"'And Madame Blanchard is not in your confidence? Does your mother know?'

"'God, no! I cannot bring myself to tell her.'

"'And de Frontenac,' I suggested, as tentatively and delicately as I could. 'Did you tell him?'

"'I sent word to his servant, that I wished to speak with him, but the servant returned with a missive from his master that he had no interest in any further intercourse with me, and that he would not receive any further messages from me to him.'

"'So he doesn't know you are with child?'

"'Against his instructions, I sent a note, confessing all, which was returned with the protestation that his lordship does not even know me. His servant warned me that if I persisted in pursuit of either his heart or his fortune, his master would denounce me in the highest circles as a pathetic little drab and a whore.'

"The words came choking from her throat, with a sickly, rasping sound, followed by a flood of heaving tears.

"'Though I may burn in hell, I'll slit his throat. I will disembowel him and hang his private parts for public display,' declared the distraught Testagrossa, his clenched fists raised to the air above him.

"'Enough, my friend, I pleaded, all the while trying to lower Testagrossa's arms to his side. 'Our first concern is with Caterina and the child, and for tonight, there is nothing to do but to keep this to ourselves... Caterina, go back to the kitchen, and no tears in front of Marie or any of the cooks or servers. Bernardo, come with me and we will plot our revenge together.' I put my hand on my friend's large, bear like shoulder, but Testagrossa shrugged it off.

"'No, unhand me! I know what I must do!' With that, he pivoted on his heels and ran off into the night.

"I was certain that Testagrossa would try to find and kill de Frontenac, and probably get killed himself in the process, the big fool!

"Caterina must have been thinking the same thing, for after only a moment's hesitation, during which she glanced at the restaurant's service entrance for perhaps the last time, she turned and ran down the hill to intercept and stop the man who loved her enough to die for her.

"Then I sprinted around the corner of the alley, hoping to still be able to see Bernardo and Caterina heading down the *Montaigne Sainte-Geneviève*.

"Sure enough, I saw a lumbering, bear-like silhouette and her slender shadow moving somewhere between a fast walk and a trot towards the foot of the slope, where *blvd Montagne Sainte-Geneviève* intersects with *rue Traversiere*. I broke into a trot, to cover enough distance to keep the two figures in sight but not to get close enough for them to realize they were being followed. Half way down the boulevard, I slowed a little, to keep my distance, and only then heard my name being called from behind.

"Without breaking my stride, I glanced quickly behind me and saw two figures heading toward me at a full run. A minute later, Dormoy and Gaudin had dropped to a synchronous jog, positioned on either side of me. Gaudin suggested that we draw back some more, since three pursuers were easier to spot than one. At the same time, the shadows were deepening, and we risked losing sight of the two figures in the encroaching obscurity ahead, if we did not keep up. The lumbering giant and his shadowy companion must have been deeply engrossed in conversation, however, because neither of them showed any sign of awareness of their pursuers or anyone else in or near their path.

"When they reached the intersection with Rue Traversiere, the figures stopped for the first time and looked about. I was certain that Testagrossa would insist on continuing straight to *Maubert*, thence to the *Pont St Michel*, the *Isle de la Cité* and the Right Bank, but instead, he turned right onto *Rue Traversiere*.

"'That's away from the river - and away from de Frontenac!' I pointed out, panting breathlessly. The three us ran the rest of the distance to the intersection and looked right. The twin silhouettes were nowhere to be seen. Had we been spotted? Abandoning all pretence of stealth, we sprinted down the *Traversiere* to the corner, where there was only a narrow alley to the left and a wide street to the right which cut back, paralleling the *Montaigne Sainte-Geneviève*. We looked to our right, and there were the two shadows, doubling back in the direction they had come. It was then that the two figures looked around, spotted their pursuers and, turning back, continued their course in the direction of the *Ecurie* and the Abbey of *Sainte-Geneviève*.

"Testagrossa and Caterina did not seem to care that we were dogging their steps. They strode with neither hesitation nor haste, like people on a mission who would not be diverted from its completion. They did not go back to the *Ecurie* as I had, at first, supposed that they might. Instead they headed straight for the main gate of the abbey, and, without waiting for us to catch up, passed through the oaken doors and out of sight.

"My breathless friends looked confused and totally at a loss about what to do next. I smiled and said, 'I have an idea.'"

Chapter 17
Plans for Revenge,
and a New Development

Journal Entry

"I didn't know how much either Dormoy or Gaudin knew of the situation, but they had put together that Testagrossa was very worried about Caterina and that the *Chevalier*, Hugh de Frontenac, whom Gaudin hated almost as much as did Testagrossa, was somehow implicated in all this. Their friend's pain cried out for justice, for retribution, for revenge, and it would be a potion that they would mix together.

"The three of us came to a halt beneath a chestnut tree, where the footpath from the abbey gates joined the road. By lowering my head, I required Dormoy and Gaudin to lower theirs in order to hear me. Thus huddled with them in conference, I briefly recapitulated the story, by way of prologue to what I would require of them. Then, I turned my attention to Dormoy.

"'Claude, you are in the confidence of Brother Anselm, our resident chemist. Get him to prepare for you an herbal concoction that will render our friend, the *Chevalier*, unconscious for two or three hours. That should do it, I think. It must be tasteless and suitable to be mixed with wine without calling attention to itself. Now go. Make haste.' Dormoy immediately took his leave and slipped through the Abbey gates.

"'Gaudin, you must return to the quarters of Montgomery's guards and cultivate the acquaintance of de Frontenac. Tell him that you have among your friends an English nobleman poet who can introduce him to the literary circle around Jeanne of Navarre. You told me that he's always looking to curry favour with Montgomery, and since the Queen of Navarre holds Montgomery in high regard, this might offer an avenue that he can scarcely resist.'

"'But why would he believe that I would put myself in a position to be of service to him?'

"'He's an egotist,' I insisted, 'and so imagines that everybody likes him and that those who don't know him are just dying to make his acquaintance.'

"'Why do you want to be introduced to that insufferable, arrogant overblown bag of ass wind?' asked Gaudin, still puzzled by these arrangements.

"'We will prepare a surprise for him that he will remember as long as he lives,'' I answered, rubbing my hands together in anticipation. 'Listen, I wish you God speed in your enterprise. I'll stay here to intercept our friends, when they come out. I hope Testagrossa isn't trying to get absolution for something he hasn't done yet. I'll dissuade him from his intended course by promising a revenge far more painful than death itself, and by assuring him that the *Chevalier* has already accomplished the damnation of his immortal soul all by himself.'

"With that, Gaudin made his way back to the barracks of the Scottish guard. As for me, I crouched in the shadow of the tree to await the appearance of the seminarian and the serving girl.

"It was Dormoy, however, who emerged from the abbey gate first, looking very much the self-assured alchemist that I had come to recognise of late. His smug, expression proved to be short lived, however, as I suddenly jumped out of the shadows, like the Devil himself, and caused the Provençale to stumble and cry out in panic. 'Careful,' he said, after he had recognised me and gained back some of his composure. 'You'll make me fall and break the vile that cost me so much trouble to get.'

"'You got it then? Brother Anselm gave you the potion?'

"'Yes, but only after I broke down and told him the whole story.' Dormoy was still panting, quite out of breath. 'When he found out that it was to help Testa..., I mean, Bernardo, he agreed enthusiastically, and suggested a couple of remedies before we settle on this innocent looking tincture. You know, he's mad by all the points of the compass, if you ask me.'

"'So, it's potent but not deadly?' I asked, with the slightest twinge of a scruple.

"'Wait, wait. I'll tell you everything.' Dormoy insisted, having by now completely regained his composure. 'I found him in the herb garden, Anselm, I mean, puttering away at his plants, as if they were children he was tucking into bed. He smiled broadly, when he saw me, because, I guess, he doesn't get many sympathetic listeners among his brother monks. He asked me how my research was going, if I remembered all of the classical references to an elixir of gold he had confided to me. Then he reached over to one of his family of plants and snapped off a pointed twig. "Here's rosemary," he told me. "That's for your memory." I didn't know that a bowl of gruel, with a sprig of rosemary, is good for restoring an addled memory. It calms the nerves, in any event.'

"'So what about the sleeping potion?' I demanded, with rising impatience.

"'I'm getting to it,' protested the devoted alchemist. 'Hold on, hold on. I had to ease into a discussion like that, sound casual about my request, or else he might panic and send me away. Anyway, we began talking of this or that kind of herbal remedy, and I asked him if there were a leaf or root that would induce deep and long sleep. At that, he frowned and looked concerned, thinking that my forbidden studies disturbed me and kept me awake at night, but I assured him that I was fine. I told him that I needed something for someone else.'

"'Now he knew that you were keeping something from him,' I interjected, even more impatient and annoyed. 'Well done, you dolt!'

"'Yes, yes, he was as suspicious of my motives and he was certain of my attempts to hide them from him. Well, at that point, I determined that the only way forward was to blurt out the truth. So I told him - everything – about Caterina and de Frontenac and Bernardo. He realised that our big, gentle friend was in great pain. The monk's concern was genuine. At last, he smiled and said that he knew of several herbal potions that were, at once, quick and powerful but left no lasting effect on either the body or the mind, so undisturbed were the blood's humours. I nodded in agreement that this was just the thing, so we retired to his laboratory, where we concocted THIS.'

"Dormoy reached into a leather purse that was tied to his belt and pulled out a small vial, stopped with a tiny piece of cork. Inside the vial was a small quantity of transparent liquid, roseate in colour, like a swallow of watered-down wine.

"'Just three drops of this in a cup of wine is enough to send anyone who drinks it into a deep, death-like sleep, from which the blare of military trumpets would be insufficient to wake him.'

"'How long will he sleep, thus?' I asked, my head lowered, the better to gaze into the tiny vial of mischief.

"'Three, perhaps four hours,' speculated the alchemist, with the air of an expert on this sort of thing. 'Then he will awaken, calm, rested and in full possession of his faculties.'

"'Perfect,' I said, gently taking the vial from between Dormoy's outstretched fingers and securing it around my waist. 'We meet again tomorrow night at the steps of *Saint-Séverin*. You must be ready to carry a load and to be as unobtrusive about it as if you were transporting a slab of beef from the market. Until then, tell NO ONE of our enterprise.'

"'Of that, you may rest assured,' said Dormoy, who appeared to relish putting on the mysterious and equivocal look of a practised alchemist.

"Thus wrapped in his palpable cloak of mystery, Dormoy headed back down the *Montaigne Sainte-Geneviève*, soon to be swallowed by the shadows of the streets below. I returned to my position, beneath the chestnut tree, to wait, once again, for the wounded giant and the woman for whom he was willing to kill.

"I was not long disappointed, for presently, the great doors opened again to emit a tunnel of light, within which the large bear-like figure of Testagrossa, the thin figure of Caterina and a taller, heavier robed figure could be discerned. The monk had a hand on each of the young peoples' shoulders, and the young seminarian had taken on a completely different aspect from that of the skulking figure who had entered the abbey not an hour before. He stood straight, to his full height, and his face showed none of the fury and frustration that it had worn before. He looked calm and resolute and dead sure of his every step. It was as if, I thought, a man had emerged in place of the confused and angry boy who had gone inside.

"As they got closer, I could see that the monk was smiling, even joking, and that Testagrossa and Caterina were smiling back, as if nothing, any more, were wrong. Caterina spotted me, standing alone and looking, I suppose, quite baffled. She raised her hand in greeting and beckoned me to their side, as if to confer some confidence.

"'Henri, we were just now talking about you. Please, please come here; we have something to tell you.' I approached tentatively, uncertain as to whether my friends had, perhaps, taken leave of their senses, so radical was their change of mood and aspect.

"'You must stay with me tonight, Bernardo, and not think of going to the right bank. Leave this in my hands. Don't do anything that you might regret.'

"'I shall never regret what I am about to do, for as long as we shall live,' said Testagrossa, wearing a smile that seemed to say that nothing that had transpired that afternoon had, in fact, really taken place. He looked as if he, himself, had taken one of Brother Anselm's mind altering herbal potions and was somewhere other than in this world of tangible things.

"'Are you quite all right?' I asked, not knowing whether to partake of the laughter or to empty a bucket of water on my friend's head to bring him back to reality.

"Caterina tried to reassure me that they were not at all mad – not in the conventional sense. 'Please, please, don't look so worried! Come, we want you to meet Father Bertrand. He's the Prior here at *Sainte-Geneviève*'s, and he's been both Bernardo's confessor and mine for two years, now. We wouldn't think of doing this without consulting him, of all people.'

"'Father, certainly you can't absolve him for what he is about to do, can you?'

"'You are *Henri* Howard, the English student, are you not?' The priest smiled affably, while extending his right hand. 'I find nothing requiring forgiveness in Bernardo's intentions or actions, unless courage and honesty are sins nowadays.'

"'*Henri*, I want to marry Caterina and be a father to her child, and to my greatest joy, Caterina wants this, too. Furthermore, we both want you to be our witness,' declared Testagrossa, his face absolutely radiating happiness and satisfaction.

"'Are you sure this is what you want, to be father to someone else's child? What of your calling to the priesthood? I know of no one else who would make a better one.'

"'A calling, as you say, is from God, and I am called to Caterina's side with such sweet and compelling force that no one but God could possibly be the author of it.'

"'Nothing happens to us by accident, young Howard,' said the priest, looking with approval at their Italian friend. "'There's a special providence in the fall of a sparrow." Perhaps Caterina is here to call Bernardo, and perhaps Bernardo is here for Caterina. All that we can do is to follow the voice from wherever it comes.'

"I paused momentarily, considering what Father Bertrand had said, but when I spoke, it was to Testagrossa. 'So you love her, and she loves you?'

"'I can assure you of the first part, but then, you've known that longer than I have. I've loved her ever since I first saw her at the *Ecurie* matching wits with besotted school boys and outwitting the greatest minds of our generation. And she is – how do you say, in your language – most beautified.'

"'That's a vile phrase, "She is most beautified!" I can teach you much better.'

"'Mean you to challenge my Caterina's beauty?'

"'I mean no offence, except upon your choice of words. I'm as faithful in my admiration for you, Caterina, as I am in my friendship with this big fellow, over here.'

"Caterina put her slender hand on my arm. 'Think nothing of it. There is nothing that can dampen our mood tonight, except for one rotten weed that still grows on the compost heap, but even he cannot come between me and my happiness, because very soon what was his will be ours.'

"Testagrossa kissed Caterina tenderly on the lips and, turning aside, clasped the hand of Father Bertrand in a firm grip. Turning back, he offered his arm to Caterina, and strode with new found confidence to the street that leads to the *Écurie*, there to plan how they would break the news to Caterina's mother."

Chapter 18
Sharing the Couple's Joy

Journal Entry

"I wanted to get back to my room on the St Victor, but I needed to know how Signora Botelli would respond to my friend's proposal of marriage. I didn't even bother to go down to the cave of our familiar haunt, but sat at the bar on the ground floor, next to the kitchen. I was working my way through a tankard of ale, while Caterina and Testagrossa were out back at the service entrance rehearsing what they would say, when, in a few minutes, Bernardo would take Caterina home.

"I realised that this would be a difficult conversation for everyone involved. Since Bernardo was neither an aristocrat nor a courtier, he would not be considered a suitable match by the Signora, who still dreamed of her former social status. Still, the Giambelli family fortune was not inconsiderable (far greater, in fact, than those of many of the courtiers who graced the Valois palaces). Like the Italian Queen of the French herself, merchant families were known to compensate in wealth for what they lacked in noble birth, and it was beginning to matter less and less. Maybe the old woman would come around after all.

"I fidgeted with my tankard, pushing the handle in clockwise, then counter-clockwise, circles. Finally, I could no longer stand the suspense. Leaving the tankard of ale half drained on the bar, I bolted for the kitchen and out the service door, opposite the entrance.

"It was full night, warm and humid as Paris gets, late in June. I was aware of a profound stillness, a hushed silence unbroken even by the rustle of leaves or the gentle swaying of tree branches. It was like a calm at sea, an unending moment of arrested movement, frozen as if by some enchantment, holding back the tides of mutability.

"I was out of earshot of the two silhouetted figures, hovering noiselessly, bending to each other's rhythm as they whispered hushed words that were only meant for each other. The thin sliver of the moon gave practically no light, and the lovers were like deeper shades within other shades where the shadow of the awning had moved aside to make place for them. Their dance-like movements were as something one might see upon a stage, a language of the limbs to speak the truth about the hidden soul and the throbbing heart, something as beautiful and transcendent as music itself.

"I stayed rooted where I stood, not wanting to trespass further on hallowed ground, nor wishing to profane the moment, for fear that it would evaporate, if I did so. Then the figures, hand in hand, turned toward my transfixed position. As they shortened the distance between themselves and me, they acquired faces and glowing smiles, and their arms reached out for me in yet another dance move.

"'*Henri*,' spoke the voice of Caterina, first. 'You are ever our friend, concerned and knowing all along why we suffered as we did. Join in our happiness as you shared in our pain.'

"'Have you decided to be our witness, on Saturday?' broke in Testagrossa. 'We shall exchange our vows before Father Bertrand and join our bodies, since both possess and share one single soul.'

"'I am honoured, my friends,' I replied, with a courtly bow from the waist, 'that you chose to share this moment with me.'

"'If the child is a boy, we will call him "*Henri*,"' said Testagrossa with an awkward grin on his full face.

"'No,' said I, smiling at the thought, 'He must have a good Italian name, like "Bernardo" or, "Francesco," or, if you must, "Enrico."'"

"'And if it is a girl?' suggested Caterina, timidly.

"'Then I shall call her "Francesca", because she comes with us from France, or "Christina"', because Christ, Our Lord, sent her so that we could not deny our love.' Testagrossa, once again, had found the right words.

"'By any name she will carry within her the sweetness of this night,' concluded Caterina, with a serenity and sweetness of her own that I had never before observed in her.

"We arranged to meet after Lauds on Saturday, at *Sainte-Geneviève*'s portico, and with that, I left them to return to St Victor's and perfect my plan."

Chapter 19
The Mouse Trap

Journal Entry

"Gaudin was waiting for me in our room, with good news about the progress he had made with de Frontenac. The *Chevalier* knew three things about Jeanne de Navarre: she was as committed as her mother, Marguerite d'Angouleme had been to the patronage and encouragement of young poets and playwrights, she was a sympathiser with the reformed religion and protector of its better known practitioners, and she was a patroness of the Comte *de Montgomery*.

"When Gaudin intimated to de Frontenac that he had a poet friend, who was on familiar terms with Pierre *de Ronsard*, François *de Belleforest* and others in Queen Jeanne's circle, and who was also a subject of the Protestant Queen of England, de Frontenac fairly jumped at the opportunity to make his acquaintance. Gaudin suggested that they meet in the student quarter, since his friend was an Englishman and better connected with poets than with courtiers. Accordingly, de Frontenac agreed to be at *Les Deux Ramiers*, a respectable tavern on *Rue Traversiere* at eight in the evening, the very next night.

"Everything was in motion. Gaudin would walk with the *Chevalier* from the field of *Les Tournelles*, where the tournament arrangements were being finalised, and would insure that he passed only the less disreputable streets, to insure that de Frontenac would not be frightened away from the area. Dormoy's job was to locate a table, towards the back of the dining room, so that he and Gaudin could sit de Frontenac between them. Gaudin would then encourage as much ale down de Frontenac's throat as he could. All the while, Dormoy would regale him with bogus prophesies of his future prowess with the renowned Scotsman and Captain of the Guard. At the appointed hour, I would burst in with the ravishing Julie on my arm, dressed to distract the prayers of an archbishop, but without the tell-tale trappings of her ancient profession. I was to ask Julie to conceal the vile of Brother Anselm's potion in the heavenly cleavage between her magnificent breasts, so as to play her part in the drama that was to ensue. Once the script had been committed to everyone's memories, the players were all ready for this day to finally come to an end."

***

"As the summer evening fell, Dormoy arrived early and took possession of a large, secluded table toward the back of *Les Deux Ramiers*. Gaudin and de Frontenac entered shortly before eight, in animated discussion about the up-coming tournament at *Les Tournelles*.

"'I hear the *Prince de Condé* is a formidable adversary, both with lance and sword,' commented Gaudin, while he quickly scanned the room for the location of Dormoy's table. 'He is said to be one of whom even Montgomery himself ought to beware!'

"'No, no, no. Our Scots Captain will overcome any knight in the King's service. He trained most of them, so he knows their tactics and their weaknesses. He's training me, you know, to be one of the most highly skilled and renowned of the King's retainers,' proclaimed de Frontenac as he swaggered to the table to which Gaudin steered him.

"'Still in all, I would watch out for the Spaniards and the Germans. The King is too quick to trust them, in my opinion,' added Gaudin furrowing his brow and playing the part of one in possession of some special knowledge.

"At that moment, our footsteps sounded at the threshold, and presently, I pushed the oaken door open and stood to one side for the shaft of radiant light that swept in through the open door. As if drawn by some magnetic force, all heads turned to gaze upon the source and centre of that radiance, the delicate white fingers, the hand, the sleeved arm and sloping shoulder up to which every eye in *Les Deux Ramiers* travelled as in a trance.

Her ink-black hair cascaded onto her shoulders and rippled from side to side as she walked, with a gentle undulation of her hips that ended all conversation at her approach.

"Her face was turned toward me, at whom she smiled with careless abandon and an arched eyebrow that said she knew she was beautiful and that every eye was wide with thirst to drink in her sweetness. She laughed silently at something I whispered to her, raising a hand almost in time to cover her moist rose-pedal mouth. I swept her toward my friends' table with effortless gallantry and stood directly over de Frontenac, the better to permit him to gaze up at the slim and undulating shape of the woman.

"De Frontenac looked as if someone had just shattered a wooden beam on his head. His eyes were glazed and his mouth was open, like one who wanted to speak but couldn't. He drew in breath, through his open mouth, but then proceeded to suspend all voluntary and involuntary activity, without even allowing himself a chance to exhale.

"Dormoy and Gaudin rose, at the approach of the lady, but de Frontenac remained immobile until, after Julie and I had stood there for what seemed like several minutes, he clumsily roused himself and nearly knocked over his stool in his haste to get to his feet. It was then that I noticed what de Frontenac wore, around his waist: a white scarf upon which he had affixed the salamander pin – his prize from one of his many conquests - to impress his new friends. I was thankful that Testagrossa was not there.

"No one seemed to know what to say or do next, until Gaudin broke the silence in order to make the introductions.

"'This is my friend, Henry Howard, the English poet I was telling you about, but I am afraid that I do not know who might be this lovely vision that so adorns his arm this evening.'

"I bowed and extended my hand in Julie's direction, making a most theatrical gesture. 'May I present the Lady Juliette, a bishop's daughter, as I am given to understand, whose father has bestowed upon her a rich love of learning and letters and an even richer dowry to insure a well-placed and suitable marriage.'

"De Frontenac had by now composed himself and bowed, in his turn, to both the lady and me. 'My delight in making your acquaintances is beyond my capacity to render into mere words. I relish only the gift of knowing you – both – all the better.'

"'My Lord is generous both in words and in sentiment," replied Julie, with a modest lowering of her eyes. 'May our acquaintance flower under the husbandry of thy eloquence to become a rich and fruitful garden.'

"Gaudin could see that de Frontenac was practically salivating into his tankard, and he had all he could do to suppress a sardonic burst of laughter, right in his face. Meanwhile, Julie and I continued to play him like a musical instrument. At every opportunity, I mounted praise for the lady's every ample attribute in choicest courtly prose, while the lady's practised movements and utterances tantalised and teased the young *chevalier* to a fever pitch of excitation. We talked of chivalry and jousting and the destiny of great nations and their still greater leaders, but the conversation always seemed to return to the consummate beauty and incandescent passion of the women who would inspire them to great acts. That this radiant ember of womanhood – and the generous dowry that her father evidently held aloft – might impel him to his certain destiny and ignite him in a burning conflagration was as clear and certain to de Frontenac's imagination as was the burning lust with which he now desired her.

"Finally, I drew in a breath and decided that it was time to spring the trap. I rose and looked around the table as if I were making ready to go. 'I must return to my writing. I feel especially inspired tonight,' I added, looking lasciviously at Julie.

"Dormoy push back from the table and sprang to his feet next. 'The Master has been very perturbed all day,' he blurted out, as if he had just remembered something. 'I must go to listen to him. He keeps talking about a lion, a golden cage and a wooden shaft. He says that it will happen very soon, maybe tomorrow.'

"'He's probably just got a splinter in his ass, and he needs to go the privy to pull it out,' remarked Gaudin, before remembering that he, too, needed an excuse to go. 'In any case,' he added, 'I must be off to the stables. Tomorrow will be a big day at *Les Tournelles*, the "Tournament of Peace", you know. You'd better get your sleep, my lord,' he advised de Frontenac, with a glance toward Julie.

"'But we cannot leave the lady unescorted, so discourteously,' de

Frontenac protested.

"'You are a true friend and a true knight, *mon seigneur*,' I responded, with yet another theatrical bow. 'I leave her in your capable and chivalric hands and trust her to your good offices. See to it that she is safely returned home,' I added with just a hint of emphasis. With that, we all rose, bowed and went out, except for Julie and de Frontenac.

"The *chevalier* was at a total loss as to what to do or say next, but Julie took control with all of the skill and prowess of her art. She held his eyes hypnotically fixed on hers, and although her mouth spoke words his ears heard none. It was as if her thoughts drifted into his consciousness soundlessly, like a dream, and although he had much to say to her, he found that his tongue could not utter a word. There was mention of a stable and caretaker's shack nearby, and he rose, at her command, having completely surrendered his volition to her, walking to the door and into the night as if he were in a trance.

"We three conspirators knew where the prearranged rendezvous would take place, and we hid in the bushes next to the ramshackle structure out of sight from the narrow alley that led there. The couple approach slowly, with only the whispered rustling of Julie's skirts to betray their presence. Once the *Chevalier* and his lady were inside, we carefully moved up to the shack, the better to be able to peer through openings between the boards that allowed both air and light to freely enter, although the door was shut.

"We saw Julie help the knight to recline on a bed with a hay stuffed mattress, while she artfully removed his doublet and threw it to one side. From a box in a corner, she produced a loosely corked bottle of wine and two goblets into which she poured their refreshment. She begged him to turn away for modesty's sake, while she worked with her bodice to secure the release of her tightly bound breasts. While de Frontenac's face was averted, she lifted the vile of liquid from between her breasts, uncorked it and poured the entire contents into the goblet of wine closest to the *Chevalier*.

"By the time she gave him permission to turn around, the vial had been toss aside and the goblet, she had prepared for him, was in her hand. She held it out for him, having raised it to the level of her bosom. She was Eve, enticing him with the fruit of his ruin, and the man could do nothing but desire and accept what was offered.

"De Frontenac grasped the cup, greedily, and took a deep swallow to quench the dryness in his mouth which his longing for her had evoked. Julie took her own goblet, then, and sipped daintily before sitting down beside him on the hay. Reassured, de Frontenac drank deeply again and closed his eyes to savour the warmth that he felt within him. The feeling overwhelmed him like the pounding of a wave and the pull of the undertow, and, for the life of him, he could not will his eyelids to open again. Surrendering completely to the languorous feeling that suffused his every muscle, he lay back on the lumpy mattress and slept like a spent lover.

"Julie lifted her gaze towards a large crack in the wall timbers and winked where she knew that her friends would be concealed outside. With hurried footsteps, Gaudin, Dormoy and I burst into the room, full of smiles and leers, and examined the limp body of the *Chevalier*. Satisfied that he would offer no resistance, I produced an empty burlap feed bag from the adjacent stall, which the three of us slipped around the ankles of the sleeping knight and pulled up the length of his body, like hose. After loosely tying it over his sleeping head, we hoisted the sack and balanced it on Gaudin's broad shoulders so that he could lug it like a slab of meat to its next destination.

"I suddenly remembered 'The Queen of Poison,' and, taking a few steps back toward the regally beautiful girl standing in the shadows, her breasts covered only by a camisole, I reached out to her aroused nipples, leaned into the dim shadow that surrounded her face and lingered on the soft, sweet moisture of her lips.

"It was time to move to the next stage of the enterprise. With me in the front and Dormoy in the back to balance the load, we three headed off in the direction of *Le Pont St Michel* to the *Isle de la Cité* and the grounds of the royal administrative offices. We halted at the mid-point of the bridge to give Gaudin a much needed rest.

"As I leaned over and peered into the dark, rushing waters, I thought about dumping the bundle into the muddy river beneath us. I became conscious of a smouldering fury towards this defiler of women, this pompous, lecherous spoiler, for which our sport did not sufficiently make answer. 'Still,' I considered, 'I am neither his judge nor the chosen instrument of his punishment. Besides, there would be investigations and consequences if the son of the *Comte de Nimes* should wash up dead and neatly packaged, on the banks of the Seine.' So the moment passed. I helped Dormoy to re-balance Gaudin's burden, and our little party set out to complete the crossing of the bridge.

"On the other side, there were scores of serving men and kitchen menials bringing bushels and sacks of food up to the hall, and the three of us, in ordinary street clothes, blended in with the procession. Most of the others turned toward a side servants' entrance, but we went on until we reached a small, grassy clearing on the approach to the main gate, still far to the side of the line of sight of the sleepy sentinels in the guard tower. We checked to verify that we were unobserved and eased the burlap sack to the ground.

"Despite our care, it landed with a decided thump, and we held our breaths for a long 30 seconds, fearing that de Frontenac might awaken and discover us before our sport was finished. He did not move. Suddenly, I was seized with the thought that the *chevalier* might be dead. Quickly, I untied the top of the long bag and was relieved to see that our captive's face was flushed and that he was indeed breathing softly. I let out a deep breath of my own.

"Dormoy saw my look of concern. 'How much did she give him?'

"'The whole vial, I think,' said Gaudin, also happy to see that he had not been lugging a dead man.

"The potential crisis having been averted, we set to work gently pulling down the burlap bag until it hung loosely around his ankles. Then, with even greater care, so as not to wake him, we began to remove his clothing until we had pulled off both his hose and the last of the burlap bag, first from one foot and then the other.

"I rolled the clothes into a bundle and stuffed them into the empty burlap bag. Before tossing the bag aside, however, I reached in and pulled out de Frontenac's white scarf, unfastened the salamander pin and then returned the scarf to the bag. 'This pin goes back to its rightful owner,' I said under my breath.

"Now that the *chevalier* was completely naked, upon the grass, Gaudin pulled from his waist the cask of honey that Testagrossa had permitted him to borrow (the same one that the Huguenot family had given him the day of the *St Germain* Fair), which he proceeded to pour liberally over the genitals and chest of his victim. 'By the time he wakes, every ant in Paris will be feasting on his meagre and inadequate parts,' he said to the approving grins of us all.

"Morning came early, at the end of June, so we pledged to meet at full light on the steps of *Saint-Séverin* and accompany Gaudin to the tournament at *Les Tournelles*, where he would serve Gabriel *de Montgomery* by grooming the horses and following them with his shovel. Gaudin and Dormoy headed for the bridge, hoping to get at least a couple of hours of sleep before the next day's events. Everyone had returned to his dwellings: everyone, that is, except for me. I searched the landscape till I found a lonely spot, dominated by an outcropping of rock, behind which I concealed myself to watch for the waking of the hapless knight.

"The dark of night soon turned to a luminous grey (the better to see the slumbering lump in the distance). Finally, a line to the east turned brilliant purple, then bloody red and still the drugged knight slept. Courtiers and dignitaries in fine cloths began to make their way to the hall's entrance, on early morning business, and they stopped to gawk at the naked man, covered with crawling ants. Abruptly, an acquaintance of the *Comte de Nimes* recognized him and called his name out to a companion. People began to gather around, talking excitedly. With the rising buzz and commotion, de Frontenac stirred, awakened, and carefully opened his heavy eye lids.

"He sat up, slowly taking in the scene, before emitting a scream of panic and anger. He reached for the burlap bag both to wipe away the ants and cover himself. Then he stumbled to his bare feet, one hand holding the burlap bag to his navel, while his clothes fell from the bag to the ground in a disorderly heap.

"When de Frontenac found his voice, it was cracked, shrill, high pitched and punctuated by frothing spittle. Whatever he may have wanted to say was garbled and drowned in the swirling depths of a cry such as a mortally wounded animal might emit before falling on the lance, trapped and helpless at the end of the hunt. 'N-O-O-O-O!! I'll get all of you for this. I'll hound you to the ends of the earth. My dogs will dismember you and make sport with your heads, to the end of my days, to the end of my days!'

"I leaned against the back of the rock, smiling to myself. 'This was so much better than killing him!' Then I began to wonder about what might happen next, and I decided to make my own way back across the bridge to the anonymity of the students' quarter."

Chapter 20
The Following Day,
a Great Catastrophe

Journal Entry

"**G**audin had already left for *Les Tournelles*, when I spotted Dormoy outside the old church at least an hour and a half after the ringing of Lauds. It was hours later than we had promised to meet, but neither of us was particularly concerned with punctuality, still flush with satisfaction from our victory over de Frontenac the night before.

"Testagrossa was not with us, preferring instead to spend the day with Caterina and her mother, who was warming to the idea of her new prospective son-in-law. Still, I had been able to relate the account of our revenge, and Bernardo seemed happy enough with the outcome, preoccupied as he was with his up-coming nuptials. For our part, Dormoy and I felt that the world had now been set right, and that we would enjoy this day, in honour of our friend whose life was about to change forever.

"Dormoy was excited because his master, Doctor Michel, had announced that he would attend the tournament, not publicly recognised by the notables on the dais, of course, but in the popular throng, surrounded by his disciples and admirers. Gaudin was already busy serving the Captain, Gabriel *de Montgomery*, confident that his hero would showcase his prowess at arms and his natural qualities as a leader of men.

"I loved the pageantry and colourful heraldry of the event, like a huge theatrical tableau being acted in the open air for the edification of the well born spectators and the amusement of the throng. There would be jugglers, peddlers and cut purses in the crowd, as well as copious quantities of food and drink, and I could just enjoy myself, without having to bother about anyone else's problems.

"'All of France will be on holiday,' Gaudin had promised us the night before, as always, deeming himself the well informed man of the world. 'Now that the King has made peace with all of his enemies and is ready to seal it with his daughter's virginity, gifted to Philip of Spain, we can celebrate the coming of an age of peace.'

"'I'm not sure which occasions the most celebration, in people's minds: the outbreak of hostilities or the moment they cease,' I speculated, as we were heading for the bridges that would cross to the *Isle de la Cité* and the Right Bank. 'The same people who cry bloody havoc and glorious deeds, when men go off to battle, weep for the mutilated remnant that return (or don't return), pray for the outbreak of peace and thank God when it finally comes. What is it that they truly want?'

"'They want their men to kill, but not be killed,' concluded Dormoy, in philosophical agreement. 'They can't accept that the one necessarily comes with the other.'

"The two of us made our way across the first of two bridges, depositing us on the *Isle de la Cité*, where we passed the scene of de Frontenac's fall, all the time congratulating each other for the good stout fellows we evidently were.

"In a light and festive mood, we crossed the second bridge onto the right bank and found that the whole city was turned out in one giant street fair. There mustn't have been any tin smiths or cobblers or carpenter's shops in operation that day, because the streets were filled with young apprentices and older journeymen who had evidently discarded their aprons and were out for a day of merriment and play. Musicians and jugglers set up impromptu stations, around which children and child-like apprentices gathered to be amused and awed by what they knew they would see.

"Notwithstanding the fact that the early morning hours had long passed, the crowds were still moving purposefully in the direction of the jousting field at *Les Tournelles*, where the full colour and pageantry of today's tournament had, for some time, been unfolding. All day, the event had been serving out heroes and villains, cheers and boos, glorious victory and bone crushing defeat, all free to the seething masses, hungry for the narcotic thrill of the circus.

"On this day, the King loved his people and the people loved their King and revered him as the father and protector of this great and disorderly family. He would watch with them and survey the festivities, with his Queen at his side and his mistress near at hand. They would see and cheer their champions, such as Gabriel *de Montgomery*, and they would remember stories that they would tell their children and grandchildren about the day when France celebrated the conclusion of peace with the Hapsburg Emperor and the marriage of the King's daughter with the Hapsburg King of Spain.

"By the time Dormoy and I arrived, the place was already a turbulent sea of humanity with a force and a will of its own. At the far end of the jousting field, at *Les Tournelles*, the public viewing area had been greatly enlarged to accommodate the day's augmented crowd. Even so, there was much pushing and shoving for placement, and people formed groups, the better to assert their collective right to proper placement.

"Gaudin had introduced us to the leader of such a group at one of the many minor events that were organized here for the knights in training, and we managed to find him in a place the group had wedged for itself, near to the barrier that separated the crowd from the pitch. My new acquaintances said that Gaudin had already made a tardy appearance at the stables in the ranks of the shovel brigade.

"Dormoy quickly spied a group of darkly clad youths who appeared rather out of place, not only because of their dress, but because their faces showed not a trace of the carefree, festive appearance of the rest of the spectators. In fact, their attention appeared to turn, not toward the pitch or the pennants or the pavilions before them, but to have gravitated inward toward the centre of their group, where there stood the stooped, red and white bearded figure of Doctor Michel *de Nostra Dame*.

"He appeared to be speaking rapidly and excitedly in a low voice that only a few could hear. Dormoy left Howard's side without a word and joined the tightening circle around the little man who had begun talking louder now about two lions and a golden cage and a great, great sorrow. No one around Doctor Michel seemed to have had any idea of what these words might mean, but they were convinced that its secret meaning was both profoundly significant and intended for their knowledge, alone.

"People were moving through the crowds with facts and rumours about the lists, information about who would be pitted against whom in today's contests. It had already been circulated, for example, that the young *chevalier*, Hugh *de Frontenac*, had forfeited and had been crossed from the lists. Now, the crowd was buzzing with the latest rumour, for the King, who had entered the lists himself and had already bested two of his most seasoned soldiers, was about to fight none other than his captain and champion, Gabriel *de Montgomery*!

"This would be the contest of the year, for King Henry was reputed to be a great athlete, and was, in his own day, considered something of a champion with the lance. Then the comparisons and the wagering began in earnest. True, the King is a burley competitor, and to face one's sovereign in combat must be more than a bit intimidating. Nevertheless, King Henry must have been over forty-five years of age, while Montgomery was at his peak and conditioned, as well. When you add to this the fact that the King must be tiring from his previous jousts and that Montgomery was a perfectionist, when it comes to form and technique, it must be admitted that anything might happen in such a match. It was further rumoured that the Queen had tried to dissuade King Henry from his intention, but that he had already promised the Lady Diane to wear her favour and was loath to lose face by withdrawing in the wake of public excitement and expectation. The inevitable fight promised, therefore, to be the climactic event of the day.

"Suddenly, the crowd turned as with one pair of eyes, towards the large pavilion, closest to the reviewing stand, upon which was displayed the golden *fleurs de lys* on a field of blue. From behind the flap, a knight emerged, clad in shining plate armour and carrying a helmet plated in gold around which was attached a corrugated circlet, like a crown. He raised a gauntleted hand to the crowd from which there erupted a roaring cheer with audible cries of *'C'est le Roi! C'est le Roi! Vive le Roi! Vive le Roi!'* ('It's the King! It's the King! Long live the King! Long live the King!')

"The excitement roiled back and forth as the King nodded and waved to the loudest voices in the crowd, while a squire brought forth a large, white destrier, armoured like his master and decked in royal blue with gold lilies of the valley. A stepping block was placed on the horse's left flank by a pair of pages. When a squire had firmly gripped the bridle, the two pages helped the monarch, in his heavy armour, to mount the beast. The squire then passed him his lance, which he dipped to the Queen and to the Lady Diane, to the riotous acclaim of the crowd.

"When it seemed that the crowd could take no more excitement, another figure emerged from the stables, already astride his war horse, fully armed and with spear in hand, to meet the royal contestant. He carried a shield upon which was blazoned the Scottish lion, rampant, on a field of gold. The knight was Gabriel *de Montgomery*, captain of the King's guard and the champion of the lists. The noise of the crowd was deafening as Montgomery tipped his lance to his sovereign lord. He prompted his horse into a bow, which the King acknowledged with a nod and the crowd accepted with a roar of approval.

"Both riders were guided by their respective squires at a leisurely pace around the reviewing stands before taking up their stations at opposite ends of the pitch. While his squire still held the bridle firmly, the King lifted his helmet to the flourish of trumpets and slipped it over his head, careful that the crown was sitting straight on top. The King squinted into the sun, realising at once that the gold plate of the helmet reflected its brilliance, to the excited adulation of the crowds.

"He also realised that the sun's position gave Montgomery an advantage, one that King Henry must endeavour to neutralise, to insure that he does not avert his eyes at the wrong moment. He lowered the visor, to see if this would help, and adjusted his vision to ignore the rows of protective grate that fell across his visage like the bars of a cage or a prison cell. He turned his head to find the most comfortable position and thought about manoeuvring the charge to favour that side view of his opponent.

"Both riders stooped to seize the reins and manoeuvred their mounts to the desired starting position. Upon a signal from the Master of Ceremonies, they couched their lances and waited for the flag to drop. The crowd fell into a hushed silence, except for a cry from the midst of a dark robbed patch of spectators.

"'The young lion will slay the elder, with a wooden shaft through a golden cage.' The sound originated from a muffled, hysterical, high pitched voice, in the midst of the crowd. It faded into silence as the flag dropped and the war horses were kicked into thunderous motion.

"The combatants, who had studied how to look for any momentary vulnerability in the opponent's technique, braced for contact and took aim squarely at the other's shield. A strong enough hit, born along the full length of a lance, might be enough to unhorse a man, but both of these men were skilled at parrying such blows, with the slightest of turns, of man or horse, at the appropriate moment.

"Seconds before the thud of collision, however, Montgomery noticed that the king had leaned forward ever so slightly in his saddle, so as to shield his eyes from the sun while keeping his line of sight aimed directly at his adversary. Instinctively, the Captain of the Guard elevated the point of his lance by the smallest fraction of an angle and turned his war horse into the path of his royal opponent.

"Montgomery's lance struck first, but not at the centre of the king's shield. Instead, it glanced across the top and kept moving until it contacted his helmet, splintering on the grating of his visor.

"The sound was like the snapping of a bent sapling in a gale. The King twisted in his saddle, under the force of the blow, his head and neck seeming to contort in the opposite direction from his massive torso. His own lance fell loose from his gauntleted hand, and he released his hold on the reins, the better to reach for his head in screeching agony. Then, in an instant, he slumped and fell to the ground like a heavy sack of grain, motionless and bleeding profusely through the gap in his helmet, from which splintered shafts of wood still protruded.

"I was conscious of an almost total cessation of sound. No one seemed even to be breathing, as figures moved with mime like steps from the reviewing stand to where their sovereign lord and master lay still and bleeding on the ground. A squire seized the reins of the King's charger to keep the panicking animal away from his master. Montgomery dismounted and fairly tore his helmet and armour from his body as he threw himself to his knees before the King's motionless form. Then the King was seen to stir and the Captain began to weep, like a child.

"At that point, the pantomime was over and someone was heard to cry:

"Physician...Bring a physician! Clear the way for the King!" Someone came with a litter, but the King waved him away. Outstretched arms lifted him to his feet while others held his head and supported him with their shoulders under his arm pits.

"Half on his own power, the King hobbled from the field amidst cries and prayers. The golden crowned helmet was tossed to the ground, as they approached the steps of the residence at *Les Tournelles*, and I caught a glimpse of the King's face, a puffy mask of blood and splinters.

"Then, chaos erupted. No one knew what to do next. The Duke of *Guise*'s mounted soldiers poured out from the recesses of the grounds and began shepherding the crowd with their lances. Someone said that the King was surely going to die; others murmured that he was dead already. The milling lost souls began to resemble a depiction of the end of the world, and someone said they had seen Montgomery running like Judas Iscariot from the Garden of Gethsemane. Someone else said that they had seen Doctor Michel and his dark clad disciples moving away on the outside of the crowd like a dark jelly fish, as far from the soldiers of *Guise* as they could get.

"'Disperse...Disperse,' was the terse command that sent them running and pushing into surrounding streets and alleys. I had long since lost sight of Dormoy, as he was swept by the swift human current in which I, myself, was trapped, down past the Celestines and closer and closer to the river. Everyone seemed to want to get out of Paris, as if the earth were about to open up and swallow the city, but I was sure that safety lay on the other side of the Seine. I moved with the crowds as it rolled and coursed through the city like flood water, moving ever down, down toward the river.

"The amorphous mob pushed past the bridge that led back to the *Isle de la Cité*. Like a body of water out of control, we rushed away, following the serpentine river to the south and west, away from *Les Tournelles*. We were stepping over people who had fallen or had been pushed down in our path: the elderly, young children separated from their mothers and screaming hysterically for someone who was no longer there. I wanted to stop to at least pick up the children and bring them to safety on the side, but the crowd kept driving me inexorably forward through strange and twisted streets I had never visited before. This wasn't the way home; it was just the way out.

"A bridge...we saw a bridge and knew with the uncanny instinct of a hunted animal that it was the way to safety on the other side. Would it hold the weight of all of these people trying to cross? Would I be shoved into the river, so that other people might pass me?

"I wasn't given any choice. I was part of the animal, and the animal was crossing that bridge. Safety...safety was in sight, but not yet under foot, and I moved, my feet sometimes lifted off the ground, until I was deposited, like a sack of flour, on the other side.

"Then, and only then, did the crowd begin to disperse, and I suddenly noticed that it was beginning to get dark. I darted into a narrow network of alleys that led more or less eastward, back toward the University and the rue St Victor.

"Alone, parched, hungry, tired and more frightened than I had felt since the day my father was arrested, I stumbled across the threshold to the welcome sight of Mme. Beber. Although I ate ravenously, I didn't taste a morsel, nor did I say anything that might disturb the hushed mood of the sullen, folk also huddled over their evening stew.

"After dinner, I went wordlessly to my room, but I could not sleep. I sat on my bed, while the shadows of evening lengthened and darkness slowly gripped the outer air itself. Lying still on my bed, I tried to comprehend the enormity of what had just happened. I had seen this giant of a man struck down, his visage covered with blood, his crowned helmet fallen to the ground like a severed and discarded head, destined to be crow's food on the end of a bloody pike! My imagination swam and swirled in the currents of my thoughts, although I tried to force myself to think no more of it. 'He's the King. He'll recover, laugh it off and give Gabriel *de Montgomery* a brotherly clap on the shoulder, or maybe he won't. God knows what will happen next!'

"The black of night was already beginning to glow a lighter grey before Gaudin finally stumbled into the room, looking as if he had run all the way home, without stopping. He spoke between gasps, as if he simply had to tell someone and I was his audience, for the moment.

"'He's hurt bad, very bad. The doctors are already butchering him, then bleeding him and applying ointments to his head. One of the maid servants came to the stables to see her lover, but they only talked and talked about what was going on upstairs.

"'There were two big splinters, the size of boning knives. One was lodged in his temple and the other looked as if it had pierced the socket of his left eye. He was conscious and he cried, when they pulled the splinters out; the King cried. The Queen has refused to leave his bedside. She was rampaging for Montgomery's head, but the King would have none of it. They were all there, *Guise*, the Cardinal of *Lorraine*, *Montmorency*, *Coligny*. All of them were like vultures waiting to feed and to tear at each other when it was over!'

"'Sit down,' I said, genuinely worried that my friend might go mad with grief and anxiety. 'Try to get some rest.'

"'The Captain spent the night in prayer, or meditating on the gallows, even though the King himself forgave him. I don't know what he'll do, if the King should die!'

"I was suddenly overtaken by an uncanny and powerful feeling, and I remembered with horror when I had last felt like this. I was certain, unshakeably certain that the King would die, just as I had known that my father would die when the soldiers took him away in the middle of the night, in answer to the summons of another King. Was it treasonable to contemplate the death of the King? Had it been parricide to contemplate the death of my father, that night, eleven years ago? Could thinking about it somehow make me responsible?

"'No,' I thought. 'I mustn't dwell on this, or it will make me mad!' I looked for something, anything else to think about. Suddenly remembering another friend, I turned to Gaudin. 'Have you heard from Dormoy?'

"'Not a word. They say that Doctor Nostra Dame has left the city, to avoid *Guise*'s net, and that his most devoted disciples went with him. I'll wager that Dormoy is among them,' he added with only the slightest hint of concern in his voice.

"I shook my head and wondered aloud if we four friends would ever be together again. From my window, I could see some children in rue St Victor, below, playing in the early morning sunlight. They had formed a circle, by holding hands, and were moving faster and faster in that circle, while singing a little rhyme that they had either heard in the street or had made up themselves, to mark the occasion. I listened carefully to their singing:

"*Le Roi de France a pris une chance,* *Ou est-t-il, maintenant?*'	(The King of France took a chance. Where is he now?)

"They fell to the ground in unison and laughed at their own cleverness. I realised that they must hear very little of anything else at home, now, and that to be able to laugh about it is a blessing only for the very young. I would not be the one to take away their mirth.

"I turned toward my friend, who had fallen totally silent (which was unusual for Gaudin). 'Will you be at the Abbey on Saturday for the wedding?'

"'Without fail! To see Father Testagrossa become Testagrossa the father is a sight I wouldn't miss for the world,' Gaudin retorted, with some of his old bravado. 'I hear we're all going over to the *Ecurie* with the blissful couple afterwards for a farewell feast, before they leave for Italy.'

"'Yes,' I said, smiling for the first time since Gaudin had walked into the room. 'I think I'll bring along Julie, if I can get her past Mme Blanchard.'

"'Will you take her to the church?' Gaudin was evidently relishing the idea of the sight of her in the midst of the holy monks.

"'Why not? She works in front of a church every evening, and it's fine work that she does, too. I can attest to that!'

"So the mood lightened for a time, although the criers continued to bellow bulletins about the King's condition five times a day, and the churches were packed with parishioners praying for his speedy recovery."

Chapter 21
A Moment of Joy
Amid Tragedy

Journal Entry

"The abbey church at *Sainte-Geneviève* was decked out, that Saturday morning, as if in preparation for Easter Mass. Brother Anselm had brought in flowers from the monastery gardens with which he had adorned both the altar and the arches all along the nave. The July sun washed much of the church in light, filtered by the blues, reds and yellows of the tall and majestic stained glass windows. Sections not already illuminated by sun light were haloed by the light of dozens and dozens of candles from which rose, like incense, a fresh perfume of bee's wax. The fragrance of the candles was transported by small wisps of smoke that emanated from the tiny caps of light and permeated the vaulted space like culinary aromas.

"I stood with Testagrossa at the head of the nave, just outside the low barrier that separated the sanctuary from the transept and nave of the church. We looked like clerics in our formal, black academic robes, freshly washed and pressed for the occasion by Mme Beber. The monks processed into their stalls, their hands tucked into the sleeves of their habits, their voices joined in a '*Te Deum*' that reverberated from the high ceiling and walls – the crystal clarity of monophonic measures ringing from human voices without instrumental accompaniment.

"Prior Bertrand emerged from the sacristy, his habit cover by a white alb, and his white, priestly stole on either side of which were embroidered a pattern of blue and red crosses. Two acolyte monks emerged from either side of the transept and opened the gate of the barrier. The priest passed through the gate and beckoned Bernardo and I to join him in the middle. Then Caterina came forward, with Marie Blanchard and Julie behind her, holding the long train of her dress, which was of fine white linen with a blue silken sash cascading from her shoulder, across her bosom and waist, then gathered around her hips. The sash was held in place by a golden pin upon which was emblazoned a shield depicting a white salamander on a field of golden flame. Around her red flowing hair, Caterina wore a crown of fresh garlands, and it seemed that there were flowers everywhere, in her hair, on her wrists, at her waist and around her hips.

"Now the organ vibrated and voices were raised in psalms of joy. I looked toward the choir stalls and saw Brother Lawrence, the librarian, towering over his fellow monks, a devilish grin lighting his face. Signora Botelli sat at the front weeping dramatically. I could not tell whether she wept for joy at her daughter's happiness or because she would now never have a titled nobleman for a son-in-law. The couple beside me, however, was oblivious to the torrent of tears.

"We listen as Father Bertrand spoke to them about how their happiness and love were ordained by God. Turning to Bernardo, the priest reminded him that God made woman from the beginning to be man's equal, his companion, his greatest challenge and his noblest calling. He turned to Caterina and told her that St. Paul had written how love is patient and kind and that it never takes pleasure from others' short comings. Looking at them both, he reminded them that love bears all things, believes all things, hopes for all things, endures all things, and that such a love never fails. With these words still reverberating from the high domed ceiling above the altar, Bernardo and Caterina repeated their vows and joined themselves in the warmth and moisture of a lingering kiss.

"With that, the monks' choir burst out with "*Jubilate Deo*", as the couple, followed by the whole congregation, processed out of the Church into the full brightness and oppressive humidity of that day in July. Everyone gathered around them to congratulate them and give them encouragement.

"Brother Lawrence, still grinning conspiratorially, reached inside the folds of his sleeve and pulled out a hand copied collection of the poems of Catullus. 'This is for you and your little sparrow, and so that you will remember our library with pleasure,' he said, pressing the little book into the bridegroom's hands.

"When it was Brother Anselm's turn, he looked uncharacteristically shy and uncertain. He ushered Bernardo a little to the side before untying a small purse from the cord around his waist. What he pulled out of the purse and held between two fingers was not money, but a small vial, containing a clear, blue tinted liquid.

"'What is it?' asked Bernardo, a puzzled and dubious expression on his face.

"'This is a distillation I prepared from a particular recipe of herbs that I've been cultivating for some time now. According to the authoritative compendium of Claudius Galen, prepared for the Emperor Marcus Aurelius, this is supposed to – how shall I explain it? – enhance the libido! I don't know if it really does what Galen claims it can do. Naturally, I could not experiment with it on myself or any of my brothers, but I thought, if you could give it a try and write to me about the result, I'd really appreciate knowing whether it actually works or not – for purely scientific reasons, you realise.'

"'Of course...thank you,' said Bernardo before turning to look at how his wife looked absolutely radiant in the sun. 'Only I don't think that I shall really need it or that using it will make much of a difference,' he added with a broad grin of satisfaction.

"'Just so, just so,' replied Brother Anselm, also glancing at the lovely Caterina. 'I'm sure that you're right about that. God bless you both,' he added with a brotherly slap on the young man's shoulder. Bernardo turned to re-join his bride, and Anselm tucked his hands back into his sleeves and walked back toward his brothers.

"Everyone but the monks agreed to meet again that evening at *L'Ecurie*, where Marie Blanchard promised a memorable feast and, as her gift to the bride and groom, all the wine that the company could drink. Gaudin promised to use all of his contacts to try to track down Dormoy, and Marie assured Julie that no comments about her profession would be tolerated that evening, either from staff or guests, so long as she remained on my arm. I assured her that this was a requirement about which I was quite content.

"I wanted to begin my guardianship right away, but I had to return to the rue St Victor alone to complete a project that had been rattling inside my head for several days, now."

"Sometimes words came easily to me, the right words in the right sequence, the cadences and the evocative scintillation of the sounds. All of this was to the craftsman of language what brush strokes are to a painter or the contours of marble to a sculptor, but these words were already tied and bundled in the bonds of friendship and genuine admiration. How does one shape what already has line and form, colour what already has tint and shade? How can one make the music new, when the melody is already resonating in one's mind? I had to put pen to paper and finish before this evening.

"Alone, in my room, above the public house that made up the bottom floor of the *Collège du Cardinal Lemoine*, I put the finishing touches on my work:

'Hath sultry summer sought two souls to bind,
Alike the slaves of Fortune's cruellest pain?
Is there no tender breeze of gentler kind,
To wipe their tears and bid them hope again?
Why must they pine in such o'er hanging grief,
Beneath the weight of calumny and loss?
Is love to kindly spirits but a thief,
That steals away the gold and leaves the dross?
No, you have that which suffering will not quell
And passion strong that tempests cannot drown.
Your love for untold ages men will tell
Your names inscribed in tales of great renown.
All future lovers for your names will yearn
Since Love's immortal laurels you did earn.

"'Now, I was ready to join my friends in boisterous celebration, having found a way to confer nothing less than immortality on Bernardo and Caterina. That was my plan, in any event, but I actually had no idea how the couple would react to my sonnet. 'After all,' I thought, 'neither of them understands English, except for a few words, which were about as much as I understand of Italian.' I considered that I should have written them something in Latin, in the style of Catullus, but only Bernardo would really be able to appreciate that.

"Then I wondered, 'am I really writing for them, or am I writing for myself?' A writer needs an audience, or else he's just a drunk stumbling out of a tavern, deep in conversation with himself. He might have something to say, but no one's listening.

"Later, there would be more time to consider such questions, but now I had to hurry to *L'Ecurie* where there would be feasting and merriment, if only for one evening in the face of an uncertain future."

Chapter 22
Festivities that End in Tragedy

Journal Entry

"**D**aylight was still asserting its dominance into the evening, but the cave of *L'Ecurie* needed sconces of candles to create the artificial everlasting twilight that hovered there. There was a long table at the far end of the room, opposite the spiral staircase, where the places of honour were set. To one side of the bride and groom sat Julie and I, while Paul Blanchard and Marie (to be served this evening) took the corresponding, opposite places. There were two chairs on each end, one of which was occupied by Gaudin, all the while surveying the proceedings with a self-satisfied grin on his face. The other chair, no doubt reserved for Dormoy, remained vacant, ready for the visitation of a ghostly spectator. A near-by table was shared by Madame Beber and Signora Botelli, both dressed in their finest and cloaked with every inch of dignity that they could summon for the occasion.

"The remainder of the tables held students and masters who had either been acquainted with Testagrossa or had frequented the establishment and were favoured to have been served by Caterina. There were musicians passing among the tables, amidst much laughter and applause. They criss-crossed between the servers who kept a continuous procession of platters and steaming bowls of savoury mutton and pork, with potatoes and carrots and cabbages combining fragrances which filled the vaulted room. The wine goblets, of course, were kept constantly full, notwithstanding the fact that the revellers were spilling almost as much as they drank, especially as the drinking continued.

"Caterina still wore her crown of laurels, although the flowers about her bosom, waist and hips had been discarded. Her deep blue eyes were wells of warm contentment and peace, as she realised what it was like to look upon and be regarded by the people in this room as their mistress, rather than their servant. I noticed her expression, and I thought she might agree that it would be a good thing if masters and servants could change places every once in a while and see the world from each other's perspective.

"Caterina glanced at her mother's table, and the two women's eyes met across the short distance between them. Her mother's expression softened with approval, for the first time, notwithstanding that there was no *chevalier* and no courtly position or title. They exchanged assurances of happiness, assurances that they each needed from the other.

"I turned to Julie and placed my hand on hers. There were no distinctions or barriers of shame between any of us this day, and I thought that there might be a chance for the future. If this is not who we are, it is, at least, what we are capable of becoming.

"I was startled from my reveries by the racket of leather heels pounding the spiral stairs like drum beats. All eyes turned in the direction of the noise and saw five well-dressed youths turn one after the other from the base of the stairs to face the company. They each had a sword, clanking in scabbards at their sides. In front stood Hugh *de Frontenac*, who drew his sword and brandished it in the direction of the head table. 'You have wronged me, and I demand satisfaction,' he bellowed to the assembled guests. 'I and my four companions stand ready to exact satisfaction from those of you who saw fit to make sport of me. Howard, Gaudin step forward and face me like men.'

"Testagrossa was the first to rise from the table, still smiling and unwilling to relinquish the open spirit of the evening. '*Chevalier*,' said he, his right hand outstretched and open. 'My wedding day is not for quarrels or ancient grudges. Either join us in a cup of wine or depart and foment your quarrels elsewhere.'

"'I'll make your wife a widow before I drink your Latin scholar's health or wish you anything but plague and disaster.'

"'Put up your sword before I shove it down your arrogant throat,' broke in Gaudin as he rose to confront de Frontenac with nothing more than his fist and a table knife.

"'We can settle this like gentlemen, outside, each with proper swords,' I added, after having risen to restrain Gaudin by both hands.

"'You are no gentleman, Worshipful Howard. What would your noble family think of the drab with whom you keep company?'

"Testagrossa moved to place himself directly in front of Gaudin and me, still trying to deflect the imminent conflict. He placed his bulk between the sword point and the rest of the company, still raising his hands in a plea for calm. Suddenly, we were interrupted by the cacophony of what sounded like hundreds of church bells tolling slowly and steadily, causing such a din that everyone was momentarily distracted; everyone but de Frontenac.

With the moment thus frozen, like a theatrical tableau, de Frontenac thrust his sword point under Testagrossa's extended arm and into the fleshy part of Gaudin's shoulder. I saw my wounded friend slump to the ground. I gave a savage cry, through clenched teeth, and raised a chair with which to beat down de Frontenac, when a cry of 'Hold,' issued from the top of the spiral staircase.

"Down stepped a crier, flushed and winded with the news that was now rampant in the streets. 'Desist for the love of God, if you have discretion and sensibility in your hearts. The King is dead. France has lost her father and her lord.'

"Suddenly, everything else was forgotten and people issued up the stairs and out into the street in panic and in search of either confirmation or denial of the news. I dropped the chair and stooped to cradle Gaudin's head, lifting him gently out of the pool of blood that was spreading from the side of his doublet. I tried, unsuccessfully to stem the bleeding, and my friend's breathing was slow and shallow. Bernardo turned to shield his wife, and de Frontenac stood still, his sword having forgotten its purpose. I looked up and fixed my gaze with undisguised fury at the motionless *chevalier*. De Frontenac's haughty condescension answered for him.

"'My father's ally, the Duke of *Guise*, will soon take control of this city for the *Dauphin*. He will rid the city of subversive and disreputable elements. My father will denounce you, Howard, as a foreigner and the subject of a heretic queen. The Duke will hunt you down and rid us of you and your kind.' With that, de Frontenac sheathed his sword and, turning without a glance toward the wounded student, he gathered his friends and remounted the stairs, amid the heavy pounding of boots.

"Julie and I helped Gaudin up the stairs and outside. We agreed that his condition called for the ministrations of Brother Anselm, rather than surgeons of the sort that had most likely killed the King. With the help of the Blanchards and some sturdy kitchen staff, we got him on a litter and carried him directly to the Abbey of *Sainte-Geneviève*."

Chapter 23
The End of a Story
and the Beginning of a Journey

Journal Entry

"**B**rother Anselm emerged from the monastery infirmary looking tired but satisfied with himself. He spotted me slumped in a corner, passing the time by scribbling my random thoughts in this small leather bound journal.

"'Your friend is going to be all right, but he's lost a lot of blood and needs his sleep right now. The wound was deep, but there was nothing vital in its path. I applied an herbal balm to prevent swelling, but it will be a couple of weeks before he can comfortably use that arm again.'

"I exhaled and my shoulders released their imaginary burden. 'Thank God! I thought we were going to lose him.'

"'Oh no, he's still got quite of bit of fight left in him, but I suggest we leave him here, under the protection of the brothers, until he's well enough to travel and take care of himself.'

"I was grateful. It seemed that the circle of my friends was in danger from all sides. I knew that Bernardo was already on his way to the safety of Italy with his new wife and mother-in-law, but I had heard nothing, for several days now, concerning the whereabouts of Dormoy. I wondered if Gaudin had said anything to Brother Anselm about their Provençal friend.

"'As a matter of fact, he rambled on about many subjects, before his fever broke. He talked about an alchemist who is a follower of Doctor de

Nostra Dame. He said that a group of them were reported to have left for *Sarlat*, in the south, but no one was saying when or by what route. They were doing their best to evade detection, I understand.'

"'As best they might,' I said, remembering the dark prophesies that Doctor Michel was said to have uttered to his circle of devotees.

"'But it was England that he talked about the most. He said you have to get back there, as quickly as possible before the Duke of *Guise* lays hold of you.' Now Anselm looked at me earnestly. 'He said de Frontenac intends to carry out his threat.'

"'That vindictive little twit,' I replied, 'he's the least of my worries, right now.'

"'Nevertheless, I think it would be a mistake to underestimate his ability to manipulate the uncertainty of these times to his advantage,' replied Anselm. 'Your wounded friend was insistent that we get you out of here, as quickly as possible.'

"'If I were to try to get back to England now, how would I avoid capture along the way?'

"'I've spoken with the Prior about that, and he has prepared letters to each of the abbots and priors of the monasteries along the route. They will offer you protection, so that, if the soldiers caught up with you during the night, even the Duke of *Guise* himself would not dare violate the rules of sanctuary in order to lay hands on you. You'll be seen safely to Calais, after which you are on your own.'

"'Thank you, Brother. You've been most kind. If I can just go back to St Victor for some of my things...'

"'You mustn't go back there. It's the first place they'll look for you. We've prepared some travelling clothes for you and some bread and cheese for the journey. If you leave now, you can get to St Giles' before nightfall.'

"'May I say "Good-bye" to my friend, first?'

"'By all means, but keep it brief, for his sake as well as your own.'"

Chapter 24
Michael and Hank
Draw Some Conclusions

I took the pages back from Hank and looked at her for some kind of reaction. She looked disappointed. "Is that all? There's nothing in the journal after that?"

"I suppose he took his travelling satchel and got out of there as quickly as he could, leaving the journal behind. We know he eventually got back to England, but there's nothing more in this account to tell us how."

"But what about Julie? Did he even get a chance to say 'Good-bye' to her or anything?" Did he ever see her again?"

"If he did see Julie before he left, we have no record of it. He apparently left the diary at *Ste Genevieve's*. From there, it found its way to the church of *St Germain*, where you found it. From what I've been able to find out about Henry Howard's life, there is no record of his ever having returned to France. He did get to Italy, however, several years later. Maybe he was able to re-establish contact with Testagrossa (I mean, Bernardo) and Caterina. Who knows?"

"Damn! And it wasn't the same England he left. There was a new Queen, for one thing."

"Oh, Elisabeth was evidently quite impressed with him, at least with his writing. I think it's entirely possible that, having seen some of his poems, she considered Henry's gift worth cultivating. In fact, she took personal charge of his continuing education, and paid for him to go to King's College,

Cambridge to complete his Masters in 1564."

Hank was rummaging through some additional notes. "How did he live, I wonder? His father's lands had been confiscated years before, and there was always this business of Catholicism hanging over his head. I guess he needed to suck up to some powerful people, since he had no title, no lands and no regular source of income, other than what little he got from writing pamphlets and occasional hand-outs from relatives."

On the coffee table directly in front of me, I had left my notes that I had taken at the British Library, shortly before leaving London. I picked up the last page, still trying to make sense of it all, and pushed it into Hank's hand. "Still, he seemed to have had a guardian angel. Even when his brother was arrested for conspiring to marry Mary, Queen of Scots, and Henry was thrown into prison as a co-conspirator, William Cecil secured his release, no doubt with the knowledge and consent of the Queen. He always managed to survive, even though his family kept falling into disrepute"

"Then there was the quarrel with Edward de Vere." She turned her attention to the top of the page I had handed her. "What is this year? I can't make out your handwriting."

"1582. Something about treasonable correspondence and attendance at Catholic services, I think."

I must have been frowning, at that point. There was something about that quarrel that didn't sit right with me, and I suppose that Hank picked up on it, as well. But now, her blue eyes were flashing with a crazy kind of excitement. "Yet they couldn't keep him in prison. You told me how he wrote directly to the Queen, and suddenly, all charges were dropped."

I guess I started talking faster myself now, still trying to get the pieces of the puzzle to fit together. "I still can't figure out why de Vere brought up these old charges in the first place. They didn't stick when his brother got the axe, and they didn't stick ten years later. Why did de Vere want Howard out of the way?"

Hank put two fingers to her lips, took in a breath and then blurted out what she was thinking. "You said Howard was hard up for money, at that time. What if de Verre were providing Howard with a regular income – in exchange for his writings? What if Howard's cousin was beginning to realise what he had there and was looking for a way to publish them or sell them to one of the acting companies, as the case may be?"

"But there's no record of any such payment."

"Of course not! Howard knew he couldn't sell anything that was the work of a suspected traitor or, worse yet, a crypto-Catholic. The transactions had to be secret, and that could have given de Verre the idea that he could re-sell them as his own and make a fortune that way."

I was with her now. I could even finish her sentences. "And that's why de Verre needed to have Howard out of the way, so he could not raise any fuss about authorship.'

"But it didn't work," chimed in Hank, finishing my sentence, in turn. "The Queen let Howard off the hook, and de Vere was forced to come up with another scheme. He could still share the revenues, because he knew very well that Howard was in no position to publish under his own name, and if we're right about de Vere's having paid for the rights to the work, he could very well have demanded to be in on the deal."

I was on my feet. I couldn't sit still. "And that's how they came up with the idea of the player from Stratford!"

"Yes, at about that time, and for the next ten years or so, after having made some strategic contacts, Richard III and the other early plays began to make their appearance. They were well received by both the court and the public, and for another decade and a half Howard and de Verre rolled them out under the pen name: "William Shakespeare."

I reached again for my files and pulled out a long list. I was reading and talking at the same time. "OK, but Howard's reputation was eventually rehabilitated. I see here that he was very much in favour with James I – Yes... made Privy Councillor, Earl of Northampton, Baron Marhull, Order of the Garder and Lord Privy Seal, all in the first two years of James' reign."

"That was about the time that Macbeth appeared, wasn't it?"

"Yes, exactly, in praise of the King, the descendant of Banquo, and look," by now I was waving the list in Hank's face. "He brought Ben Jonson (one of Shakespeare's chief rivals) before the Privy Council in 1604 on a charge of 'popery' and treason for his play, *Sejanus*."

"That's a little bit like the pot calling the kettle black!"

"I guess he wanted to position himself above suspicion, but he also might have been taking a lesson from his cousin, de Verre, by denouncing a rival to get him out of the way."

Hank looked up and furrowed her eyebrows. "There does seem to be a pattern here. He was definitely out for self-advancement."

"And his fortunes just kept on rising. In 1609, he was elected High Stewart of the University of Oxford, and in 1610, the King granted him territory in Newfoundland, of all places. Maybe he was thinking of sea voyages to distant lands. It doesn't appear that he ever went there, though. He was still in England in 1612, when he was made Chancellor of the University of Cambridge."

Hank brought us back to the Shakespearean question. "I guess he was no longer hard up for money, then. So, if he was the author of those plays, why didn't he publish them in his own name now that he was on his feet?"

"Well, I guess the persona of William Shakespeare, the playwright, was pretty well established in the public's eye by then, and there was the 'Overbury Case'."

"What the hell was the 'Overbury Case'?" Hank threw her papers down on the coffee table and put her hands on her hips.

"Sir Thomas Overbury was an enemy of the Howard family that our friend brought up on some flimsy charges that got him carted off to the Tower. Then, it seems, Howard intervened to have a friend of his appointed Lord Lieutenant of the Tower and report to him regularly on Overbury's health."

"That was thoughtful of him."

"Yes, except that Overbury died there, people think from the effects of poison administered at the direction of Howard's great niece."

"The Queen of poison!"

"So there was the whiff of scandal hanging over Howard and his family to his final days. Anyway, the plays of Shakespeare were only printed individually in quarto format during his lifetime. The first collected folio was not until 1623, seven years after the death of William Shakespeare and nine years after the death of Henry Howard. "

"So they died within two years of each other?" said Hank thoughtfully.

"Yes, and the truth about the plays' authorship may very well have died with them."

"I'm still not convinced," pouted Hank, always the sceptic. "We haven't proven anything more than the de Vere people have."

"There's still the question of the sonnets," I stared at her, as if I were holding an ace in my hand. "The sonnets were published in Howard's life time, and Shakespeare's, in 1609, to be exact, at the height of Howard's favour with King James."

"You're about to tell me why that's significant."

"Yes, well they were published as Shakespeare's sonnets, of course, but the dedication page, written by the publisher, Thomas Thorpe, contains a very interesting text."

Hank reached for my notes on the table. "Show me," she said impatiently. I pulled out a page from the pile and handed it to her. It was a clear facsimile of the original I had seen at the British Library. She read it carefully, out loud:

'TO.THE.ONLIE.BEGETTER.OF
THESE.INSVING.SONNETS.
Mr.W.H. ALL.HAPPINESSE.
AND.THAT.ETERNITIE.
PROMISED.
BY.
OVR.EVERLIVING.POET.
WISHETH.
THE.WELL-WISHING.
ADVENTVRER.IN.
SETTING.
FORTH.
T.T.'

I looked over her shoulder at the page she was staring at so intently. "'T. T.'" is Thomas Thorpe, the publisher."

"And...who the hell is 'Mr.W.H.'?"

"Oh, there are any number theories about that. The candidates include: William Herbert, Henry Wriothesley (both of whom are 'lords' and not 'Misters'), William Hall, William Harvey, and the list goes on."

"But what do you think, Michael?" Her eyes were open wide and fixed on mine.

"Just possibly, ...maybe I'm crazy, but... What if 'W.H.' actually stands for the Worthy Howard, a name about which the editor would be understandably ambiguous, while wishing, at the same time, to express his gratitude to the true and 'only begetter of these ensuing sonnets'? "

"The real 'William Shakespeare!'" Hank stood there, open mouthed, not knowing what to say.

"And while the immortal (Ever-Living) Shakespeare gave his name to these verses, it was Howard who was the actual true father (the one who did the 'begetting')!"

Hank was silent for several long minutes, thinking about what we had both just said. "If you publish these findings, you'll stir up a maelstrom of controversy, you know."

"Yes," I answered. "I know."

We both needed some fresh air. I suggested we go down to the Napoleon, a little restaurant on the corner that served the most delicious blueberry pie with Chantilly cream. We felt slightly intoxicated with the excitement of what we were now both sure had been an important discovery. We talked and laughed like a couple of teenagers on our first date. After wine, dessert and coffee, we talked sentimentally about the story that I had created from the little journal.

Hank patted her lip with the end of her napkin and leaned over the table. "Do you know what happened to the others? Did Bernardo and Caterina make it safely to Italy? Did Gaudin follow his Captain Montgomery and what became of him? Did Dormoy ever turn up?"

"No idea. Of course, we know what happened to Doctor Michel de Nostra Dame. He headed out of harm's way, back to Province, where he was able to publish his prophesies without any imminent fear of harassment. There's even a story that the Queen Mother arranged to meet him, when she was on progress in the south with her son, the boy king, Charles IX. She was still obsessed with the occult and wanted to hear good news about the survival of the dynasty. It appears that Nostradamus didn't have anything good to say about anyone in the family, except for Henry of Navarre, who eventually brought an end to the Valois line and ushered in the Bourbons. Those were interesting times – turbulent, bloody, but interesting."

All of a sudden, I looked at Hank, her eyes betraying the same curiosity I was feeling myself, and I blurted out: "How'd you like to take a trip with me to Italy. We'll find the town where Testagrossa was born and look up parish records, anything that might tell us what happened to him, Caterina and the child." I was sure she'd say "No", but I'd win points for making the big move.

Hank's eyes immediately widened at the idea. "Let's DO it! There's got to be more to this story!"

My mouth dropped open. I never considered the possibility that she might say "Yes." Now I had to act as if it were the most natural thing in the world for two scholars to go on a research expedition together. "Yes, and we can look into finding out more about Gaudin and Dormoy, based on what Howard thought they were going to do. We might even be able to find out more about Howard himself."

"Easy does it, big boy, I didn't say I was willing to give up my day job for this."

I tried to be as nonchalant and reassuring as I could. "Don't worry about it. I'll get you a sign for your book store that says 'Gone Fishing' in two languages. It'll be an adventure!"

And so, our search continued for missing lives, the threads of which disappeared some 450 years ago.

Epilogue

ank and I did take a trip to Italy, and to Normandy, *Cavaillon* and *La Rochelle,* in search of the finest of threads from the past. It's amazing how time and war can erase the footprints of ordinary lives, as if they had never been there. Perhaps they erase the actual traces of great lives, as well, and because the world needs a record of such notables, we simply make up what isn't there and convince the world that what we have found is actually so. At least nobody bothers to make up things about ordinary people.

Of Dormoy, there was no trace, neither among the University archives nor the parish records at *Cavaillon,* in Provence or among the papers and effects of Nostradamus. It was as if he had simply vanished, without a trace. More likely, however, he had only taken another name, either for his own protection or that of his family, in those uncertain times. Whether he had mastered alchemy or branched off into other areas of science and ended up teaching and writing somewhere, we'll never know, perhaps.

The parish records did provide information about one person of his family, a certain Celeste Dormoy, a sister according to baptismal records, who died in 1564, during one of the outbreaks of plague, at the age of fifteen, unmarried. There does not seem to have been anyone by the name of Dormoy in *Cavaillon,* in *Sarlat* nor in any of the near-by villages, after that.

On a more cheerful note, Bernardo and Caterina were survived by five children, twenty two grandchildren and sixty-eight great grandchildren, before their church was destroyed in a fire and the records were transferred to another parish where nobody by the name of *Giambelli* was registered. Hank and I finally tracked them down in the town of *Portecorvo,* where there were no fewer than nine churches, four of which had its own set of

Giambelli family records, testifying to a family that excelled in the production of male offspring to carry on the family name.

We knew we had located our Testagrossa because this *Bernardo Giambelli* was married to *Caterina Maria Botelli*, and the two parents had presented their daughter, *Francesca Christina*, to be baptized on the twenty-third of May, 1560. The records show that they presented four other children for baptism. In her turn, *Francesca Christina* married someone named *Giovanni Petruccio* and presented her own children for baptism. The third child, baptised on April 23rd 1587, was a boy who bore the name *Enrico*, and the priest marked the register with the conspicuously English name of Henry Howard as godfather.

Gaston Gaudin, as Howard had anticipated, followed his master Gabriel *Comte de Montgomery*, when he fled the ire of the Queen Mother in Paris and took refuge in his Norman estates. Like Montgomery, Gaudin converted to Calvinism and joined the forces of *Coligny's* Huguenot army that fought against the forces of *Guise* in the Wars of Religion. Once we had gathered this from old regimental lists, Hank suggested that we simply follow the major confrontations of those wars, examining the surviving accounts about the securing of supplies and ordinance, the granting of commissions and lands, and the memorial plaques containing the names of those who had fallen in service to the cause.

This is what brought us to the city of *La Rochelle*, the scene of a five month siege lead by the King's brother, the Duke of *Anjou*. The city's defenders are said to have held out bravely, eating dogs, cats, rats and cockroach soup after the food stores had run out. I read that the defending army lost 1500 men, but the besiegers lost over 12,000 to combat fatalities, sickness and desertion, and still they held on before lifting the siege and just going home. All that death and suffering was for nothing, in the end.

Hank and I wandered the winding streets of the old city, like a couple of vacationers, taking pictures and stopping just inside the Saracen gate for an ice cream cone. We were headed for the church, which had been Protestant in the 1570s, outside of which was a large plaque covered with the names of the honoured dead, under the partially effaced date of "6 July, Anno Domini 1573." We searched through the list like a nervous mother, hoping not to find what she is looking for, and there he was: "Gaston Gaudin, died 12 June, 1573."

He must have been no more than 35 years old at the time. Hank and I looked at each other. Hank looked as if she were going to cry, but I was just angry, angry about the stupidity of it all, and then how we memorialise what we have done on plaques of stone.

We returned to Paris, and Hank suggested that we look for information on Julie, but there was nothing, no trail to follow. She was, after all, a prostitute. Howard never knew her last name. Hell, he couldn't even be sure that Julie was her real first name. She lived on the fringes of society, probably working until age robbed her of her beauty and the sparkle of her eyes. Then she was left to live in the streets, a toothless, old woman in rags begging at church doors.

That's what I supposed, but Hank disagreed with me. She insisted that the Julie of our story was captured and saved on the pages of Howard's verse, there to be kept forever young, forever beautiful, ever full of life and mischief. As long as people could read Howard's poems, Julie would never change or fade or die.

Wasn't it as the Bard himself had written?

"But thy eternal summer shall not fade
Nor lose possession of that fair thou owest;
Nor shall Death brag thou wander'st in his shade,
When in eternal lines to time thou growest:
So long as men can breathe or eyes can see,
So long lives this and this gives life to thee."

William Shakespeare, Sonnet 18

Yes, that is what Howard would have wanted for her, and perhaps he was destined to bestow this gift upon her as no one else could, before or since.

Afterward

Henry Howard, the second son of the Earl of Surrey, was an actual historical personage. His life and family background, including the execution of his poet father by Henry VIII of England, is well documented. Similarly, the personages of Michel de Nostra Dame, Gabriel de Montgomery, King Henry II of France and his Italian queen, Catherine de Medici are all true to their historical counterparts. The account of the death of the French king adheres accurately to historical testimony that has come down to us in the form of contemporary and subsequent commentary. That Nostradamus prophesied the manner in which Henry II would meet his untimely end has been duely noted, both in his own time and in the centuries that followed, as part of the legend and mystique of this controversial figure.

Apart from this broad historical setting, the other personages and events represented in this work are completely fictional, as is the present day account of finding a mid-sixteenth century journal which belonged to and was written by Henry Howard. In the diction and syntax of passages taken from the journal, I have tried to convey a sense of the richness and vitality of written and spoken language in Renaissance Europe. I wish to acknowledge my indebtedness to the great voices of that era, who have endowed us with a literary heritage marked by unsurpassed heights of linguistic virtuosity. This book is very much about language: the beauty of its texture, the force of its eloquence and the music of its cadences.

That sixteenth century students, both in England and on the continent, would have had ready access to the source material from which Shakespeare drew inspiration for many of his plots is a supposition I make without any misgivings, although in and of itself it proves nothing. I offer no claim to authority as a literary historian, nor do I seek to contribute to the on-going academic discussion of what has been called the Shakespeare authorship question. I simply ask the reader to accept this account as an imaginative story set against a real and vibrant literary and historical background.